DEADLY INN TENSIONS

NOVA NELSON

FFS Media

ISBN: 978-1-959041-07-8 (FFS Media)

Deadly Inn Tensions, The Dahlia Wildes Magical Mysteries #2 / Nova Nelson -- 1st ed.

www.eastwindwitches.com

Contents

To my familiar, Penny: Thank you for the courage.

Chapter One

Stepping outside my comfort zone was never a beloved pastime of mine, but it seemed like all I ever did lately. Since leaving behind my admittedly mundane life in New Orleans and starting over in Eastwind (totally involuntarily, by the way), there were very few things I encountered in my daily life that *were* within my comfort zone.

Among the most jarring new additions to my world were magic, genies, the Grim Reaper, and the fact that I was, turns out, a witch. Not the wand-waving kind, but a witch all the same. I could see spirits and feel emotions. And who-knew what other talents I might discover? I was advised that it could be years before I knew the extent of it.

That was the "fun" of being a Fifth Wind witch. There were so few of us that our powers weren't well catalogued and always came as a bit of a surprise once they arrived. If you were lucky, they blossomed as soon as you needed them. If you weren't lucky, they would show up at inopportune moments that left anyone around you confirmed in their belief that Fifth Wind witches were exceptionally odd.

There were also plenty of things that started outside my comfort zone but were becoming integrated into it. The pottery studio where I worked, for one. And the folks I encountered around the quaint little town every day. Atlas, the big, white hellhound who was magically bonded to me as my familiar was yet another. And the cold of a real winter.

My hope was that, eventually, working on the pottery wheel would also become part of my comfort zone.

I didn't expect that day to come anytime soon, though.

As I sat at the pottery wheel in the studio portion of Time to Kiln on that chilly Friday morning, I let my foot off the pedal, and watched the wheel slow to a stop. I tilted my head side to side, observing the ruined lump of clay at the center from multiple angles, hoping to figure out what went wrong so soon after I started working with it. My hands were already covered in a thick layer of dark slip as I studied the asymmetry of the lump.

"Keep practicing your centering," suggested the man on the wheel facing mine. "It's probably the hardest skill to learn, but it's the most valuable. If you're not sure it's centered, then it's not centered. When it *is* centered, you'll feel it so clearly that you won't even doubt it."

I sighed as I looked up at Dante Fontaine. He was trying to encourage me, and for that I was grateful. Yet it was tricky not to feel discouraged after the second failed attempt.

"Sorry," he said quickly. "You didn't ask for tips."

"No, no." I grabbed my wire tool and dragged it between the clay and the wheel to separate the lump and make way for a new one. "I clearly need as many tips as I can get."

"You should've seen Landon try this," said the woman at the wheel beside mine. "Because he couldn't calculate his way through it and make it an exact science, he gave up after a week. I've never seen him so red in the face." Grace Merryweather snickered at the memory as she pulled her clay up into an even cylinder.

It was only the three of us in the studio this morning. Well, the three of us and my hellhound familiar, Atlas, who snoozed in the corner. Despite his size, Atlas was a nervous type, but I'd found that something about the studio put him at ease. It helped that the owners, Raven and Jude, had installed a nice big dog bed in the far corner. It was less of a kind gesture and more resignation that so long as I was around, my familiar would be too, so they might as well give him a place to park away from the wet clay. Most people didn't take kindly to large white dog hairs ending up in their pots.

While Time to Kiln afforded to stay open almost entirely because of the class fees, there wasn't a morning class on Fridays, and so we had the place to ourselves. I normally spent my mornings working in the shop at the front of Time to Kiln, but Sasha Cosmo claimed the Friday morning shift (she wanted to enjoy herself in the evening), leaving me free to absolutely fail time and again at making basic bowls and cups on the wheel.

I thought I would be so much farther along after three weeks of this, but no. It was hardly fun at all yet. If

Grace and Dante hadn't joined me each week, I would've given up much sooner than Landon had.

There was a good chance they knew that, too. I suspected it was why they hadn't missed a week yet.

I scraped the wheel clean and started with a fresh ball of clay, slapping it down as close to the center as possible.

"You'll get this one," Grace said, encouragingly.

Thankfully, both she and Dante quickly immersed themselves in their own projects. Grace was making a set of tall tankards for a New Year's party she and Landon would be hosting at their house. She was on a tight schedule with the new year only two weeks away. The clay would need to dry to leather-hard before she could trim it, and then there were two firings and a glazing before they would be ready.

Thankfully, she was excellent at pottery, and she already had ten nearly identical tankard bodies lined up in a pretty little row on a table beside her. Seeing her handiwork gave me hope that maybe one day I could create something beautiful as well.

Dante was working on a teapot, and so far, so good. It wasn't one of the quaint ones I'd seen in the shop, but a much larger one. And of course it was. The werebear was all brawn, and the idea of him pinching the little handle of a teapot to pour it was ridiculous and impractical. Apparently, werebears were not known to be gentle or delicate.

"Is that for you?" I asked.

He didn't look up from the wheel as he said, "No, it's a gift."

"For the holidays?"

"Yep."

"Speaking of the holidays," said Grace, "I heard Ellie Stormstruck and Sam Hopflora are spending winter solstice together in Avalon."

Now Dante looked up. "Really? But I thought Sam was dating Bonnie Bingham."

Grace grinned. "Apparently not."

"What happened?" he asked.

I laughed and listened along, only vaguely aware of the people included in the gossip.

This was what I loved about the studio. It was a bubble of a place, overlooked by most Eastwinders, but a fantastic way to catch up on the gossip. When I first met Dante—my heart flutters even thinking about it—I had pegged him as more of a strong, silent type. Maybe a little bit of charisma when needed. But in the time we'd spent together since he'd opened up about his feelings for me, I'd seen so many other interesting parts of him. He was strong, sure. Silent when he wanted to be.

But he was also talkative, effusive, warm, honest, and occasionally a shameless gossip. Grace, who appeared to be more of a bookworm than a gossip in any other setting, seemed to bring it out in him here. And perhaps he brought it out in her, as well. Or maybe the studio brought it out in everyone, like all great community spaces do.

I felt lucky to be included in their existing friendship, and I enjoyed the enthusiasm and animation of their updates.

But when the conversation turned more personal, I felt myself tensing up and tried not to let that transfer to my hands, which would ruin another attempt at centering.

"Landon's parents are hosting everyone for the solstice feast," Grace said. "We hosted last year, and it was a disaster. Monte had a meltdown right before the pies were ready, and I was so busy trying to calm him that the pies burned. Landon was wrapped up in mediating a conflict between his cousin and uncle, and only noticed something was wrong when he smelled something burning. The pies were a crisp by the time he got to them, and that didn't help the mood. Not that things had exactly been peachy before the baking disaster. His mother and uncle don't get along very well. Frankly, nobody gets along with his uncle, but they're all the family he has, so they keep inviting him. He cast a spell two years ago that turned all the gifts into unicorn swirls."

"On purpose?" Dante asked, laughing.

"Oh yes. He said the only thing he asked for each year was a new cauldron—he claims they cursed his current one, though he never says who 'they' are—and it was clear that none of the gifts waiting to be opened were cauldrons. So, he turned them all into steaming piles of unicorn swirls. When the rest of us explained that his cauldron was hidden in a bedroom because it would've been too obvious if we'd left it with the rest of the gifts, he didn't even apologize. He accused us of tricking him. Took us three hours to sort out what each gift was and transfigure it back. The mood was admittedly dampened by then."

Even Grace was chuckling as she retold the story, and while I could follow along, I couldn't relate. My family had never had big gatherings for the holidays. My parents couldn't afford gifts for all their children, so we usually went our own ways, embarrassed by our parents' obvious shame and trying not to bring it up to avoid making them feel worse about it. I didn't even know any of my uncles.

"What about you, Dahlia?" said Grace. "You have solstice feast plans with Nora and Tanner?"

It was a natural presumption to make. Nora Ashcroft was essentially my mentor in all the ways of being a Fifth Wind. She was the first person I'd spoken to when I wandered out of the Deadwoods, totally disoriented, and she was the first to realize what I was. She'd taken me in and offered both Atlas and me a room in the house she shared with her husband, Tanner Culpepper, one of the town's deputies. They were kind, generous people. Also, busy people. They treated me like a little sister the moment I arrived, and to be honest, their generosity often made me uneasy. I could never repay them for it, and in my experience, people always called in favors eventually.

However, if *anyone* wouldn't do that, if anyone would simply give because it was the right thing to do, it would be Nora and Tanner.

I'd heard winter solstice mentioned a few times in conversation, but I wasn't quite certain of the significance. I was getting the impression from Grace and Dante that it was a big deal, almost equivalent to Christmas in New Orleans.

Were Nora and Tanner planning to include me in their celebrations? Did I want that, or would it make me a third wheel?

"I'll probably just hang out with Atlas," I replied. "I don't really know any of the traditions, and—"

"No way," said Dante. "I'm not letting you be alone

on the solstice. It's the darkest night of the year. It's a time to spend with the people you care about and who care about you. If you don't already have plans with Nora and Tanner, you should come up to Fluke Mountain with me. We throw a big party with lots of food and drinks."

"Who's we?" I asked, my heart racing with both excitement and crippling anxiety at the thought of spending time with Dante over the holidays.

"The sleuth."

"Who?" I asked.

"Ah, right. The werebears. A group is referred to as a 'sleuth.' That means it's open to any werebears in East-wind, not just our clan. A clan is the organized structure of the sleuth," he added quickly. "Darius Pine is hosting this year at his cabin. He's the head of the werebear clan, but he's not the oldest of the sleuth. Anyway, you should come."

That old familiar feeling of being the outsider came creeping back in. "Yeah, maybe," I said, my mind already thinking of excuses not to go. "I'll have to see what Nora and Tanner have planned."

You would think being invited to a family gathering by the guy I couldn't stop dreaming about would be a win, something to look forward to. But it only scared me. I would stand out like a sore thumb there, the only witch, probably half a foot shorter than everybody else. My time in Eastwind had made it clear enough that not everyone felt as warm about Fifth Wind witches as Dante. Our powers were those of the spirit, and that included the spirit after it left the body. We were omens of death for many people, the closest thing to being the Grim Reaper himself, though anyone who took the time to get to know

Ted would understand that he was as harmless as a baby bunny.

More simply, I was just starting to feel like I fit in to certain places in Eastwind. I wasn't in a hurry to be reminded that I was an outsider. That was exactly what celebrating with the werebears would feel like, I was sure.

"You, Landon, and Monte are welcome to join, too," Dante offered. "Unless you're hoping to be there when Landon's uncle turns the whole feast into unicorn swirls this year."

Grace paused on the wheel. "Huh. Yeah, that might be fun. I'd certainly prefer something a little less prone to magical chaos. I'll ask Landon and see what he thinks."

The idea of Grace and Landon being there with their son Monte made me feel slightly better about the prospect. Grace and Landon were both North Wind witches, and Monte was a werewolf. I wouldn't be the only person there who wasn't a werebear, at least.

Sasha Cosmo stepped into the studio from the shop. "New order just came in, Dahlia."

I perked up, listening intently, though I wasn't sure why she was telling me; I wasn't working.

"It's a flower delivery," she explained. "Up on Fluke Mountain. I would do it, but someone has to watch the front desk. Because, well, you know."

I did know. A woman had been killed in the Time to Kiln shop on the same day I'd arrived in Eastwind. Jude and Raven had run a loose ship up until that point, and Sasha was allowed to work in the studio during her shift, so long as she greeted guests at the front when she heard the bell above the door. That lax approach had allowed a vengeful killer to sneak a cursed bowl into the shop, which later killed an innocent woman. Whoops!

I'd helped Nora, Tanner, and Deputy Manchester investigate the case and almost fallen victim to the same killer in this very studio. Thankfully, it hadn't soured me on the place. But I certainly wouldn't forget the importance of having someone working the register of the shop whenever it was open for business.

"So... you want me to deliver flowers?" I asked.

"Someone has to." She let the obvious implication hang.

I looked down at the clay on the wheel in front of me. Still not centered. "Can it wait fifteen minutes? I need to clean up."

She shrugged. "I don't see why not."

As I scraped the clay off the wheel and threw it back into the bag with the other failed attempts, Dante finished the body of his teapot and began cleaning up as well. "I'll walk you up there."

"Oh no, there's no need," I insisted.

"She said it's up on Fluke Mountain. I have today off work, so I was heading up there after this anyway. I can help you find the address for the delivery."

I opened my mouth to reiterate that I'd be fine, but Grace elbowed me hard in the arm. When I looked at her, she was rolling her eyes and shaking her head.

Right. I was doing it again. "Okay, if you're already heading that way," I said. "I wouldn't mind the company." It wasn't like they had Google Maps in this place. I would definitely need some help finding the address.

Why was I like this? It was as if I was actively trying to keep him from liking me. Dante was the kind of man I could only dream of, and he'd already made it clear that he cared about me in some capacity, even if I didn't have a clue as to the depth of it. Frankly, it made no sense to me.

He wasn't my boyfriend, if people even used that term in Eastwind, and we hadn't kissed or anything like that. I was starting to wonder why, while at the same time freaking out at the idea of him kissing me. It would be wonderful. Wonderful and overwhelming. Probably terrifyingly overwhelming. As a mental image of it ran through my head, a tingle went through my arms. I shook it off and finished cleaning up my wheel, which was covered in brown, watery clay.

Once we had both cleaned up and I hung my messy apron on the hook to dry, Dante and I headed into the shop.

"This one," Sasha said, handing us a tall, slim vase. The glaze was a beautiful swirl of jade green, terra cotta, and gold. A bit of detailing around the center reminded me of winter garland. "They didn't specify what kind of flowers they preferred. Just something wintery."

"That's probably all Whirligig has growing right now," said Dante.

"Once you pick out some flowers, deliver the vase to Muscoff Manor Inn on Fluke Mountain. Room"—she grabbed a slip of paper off the desk and squinted at it—"Room D."

"And who are these from and to?" I said.

Shook her head. "The message doesn't say. I received an order and payment by owl. No signature."

Dante and I shared a look. There were a thousand ways that mysterious flowers showing up at someone's doorstep could go wrong, but neither of us said that. We didn't need to. The understanding was instant.

I was suddenly glad I had a big, strong werebear accompanying me on this errand. The last thing I wanted was to be alone at the start of some lovers' quarrel.

I woke up Atlas, who was eager to join us for a jaunt in the cold weather, and then we set out with the vase.

Chapter Two

Atlas struggled with courage, as many of us do. I couldn't blame him one bit, considering the way he'd been picked on by the other hellhounds in the Deadwoods for looking different. He had a thick coat of white fur (if he'd submitted to a bath that week, otherwise it was more like beige) that made him stand out from the rest of the hellhounds. Their coats were jet black and allowed them to move around almost invisibly in the dark forest. Life hadn't been easy for him, and he'd learned to view almost everyone and everything as a threat. He'd even been scared of me when I'd first arrived, even though he was easily twice my weight.

I knew he was capable of courage, though. He'd saved me from a killer by fetching help when I'd needed it. Sure, he hadn't come charging in to tackle the threat and save the day, as one might expect a hellhound familiar to do, but courage can look all kinds of ways, and I prefer to measure it by the amount of fear one feels while doing what must be done, rather than the recklessness of the act itself.

Because Atlas lived with so much anxiety, my precious familiar showed more courage on a daily basis than anyone I knew.

Every day acts required courage from him. One day it might be letting a small child he didn't know give him a scratch behind the ear. Another day it might be passing Tanner's familiar, Monster, in the hallway without tucking his tail between his legs and rushing by. My heart swelled each time I witnessed one of these acts of bravery that others might not have noticed. I was so grateful to have him as my familiar, my partner for life. I'd only known him a matter of weeks, and I already loved him dearly.

Easily two feet of snow had fallen over Eastwind the night before, and Atlas was loving it. Finally, he blended in. If he'd laid down in one of the drifts, no one would be able to spot him. I could tell it was lifting his spirits as he trotted next to me up the cobblestone streets toward Whirligig's Garden Center on the edge of town.

Dante was on my other side, and he waved to the other townsfolk as he passed them. I was recognizing more and more faces each day. Many still didn't appear to know what to do with me, the new Fifth Wind in town.

New Orleans is a diverse city. People come from all different backgrounds, practice all different faiths, and look all different ways. My parents were different races, which might've been a problem for some folks in a different part of the country. But not so much in New Orleans. If I'd learned anything from living there, it was that the best antidote for a fear of strangers was to spend more time around them. I'd always struggled to name the differences between people. My mind just skipped over it and tended to see how everyone was the same in the important ways.

I knew better than to believe everyone's mind worked that way, though.

The only exception to my ability to see how everyone was the same was... me. And wasn't that a paradox? It was blindingly obvious to me how different *I* was from the rest of the world. Especially now that I was one of only three Fifth Winds here, and the other two had years of experience with their powers.

Hopefully, the townsfolks of Eastwind would eventually get used to me. The more they saw me doing harmless things like shopping for groceries, delivering flowers, or walking through the streets with people they already knew and trusted, the fewer and farther between those suspicious glances might become.

"I haven't been to Whirligig's since I was a kid," Dante said as a thin layer of snow crunched beneath our boots. "My mom used to take me with her. She loved having fresh flowers for the house. Still does. She grows her own now, though. My dad's happy enough about that. He told me once that he felt overwhelmed by all the selection at Whirligig's and never knew which ones to pick out for my mom. Now he can take flowers from the garden and he's sure she'll like them because she was the one who decided to grow them."

"That's adorable," I said. "It's so sweet that your father still gets your mother flowers, even if he's not going to great lengths to get them."

Dante smiled. "He's a good man. I've had to fight him a few times, but—"

"Fight him?!" I spat. "Sorry. No judgment. I just wasn't expecting that."

Dante chuckled at my reaction. "It's a werebear thing. We don't usually argue. When we're angry, we fight until we're not. We settle it there and then. Keeps grudges from building up. Not every clan encourages that, but it works well for us." He must've seen my concern, because he said, "We do it in bear form, and we have thick skin. We don't swing at each other to injure, just to blow off steam. It's mostly wrestling anyway."

I hadn't yet seen Dante in his bear form, and I wasn't sure I wanted to. Sure, I was a witch and that was strange enough, but at least I always looked like me. Seeing the guy you have a massive crush on turn into a bear is unsettling and also raises a lot of questions I was happy to put off as long as possible.

"What were the fights with your father about?"

"The usual stuff. I was a little rebellious in my teen years. Grew a big head about myself at Mancer Academy. Big fish, small pond. One of the times we fought was because I missed curfew. Dad didn't appreciate that."

"Oh. Was he strict?"

Dante chuckled. "No. Not at all. He's totally reasonable. When I say I missed curfew, I mean I *missed it*. Not by a half hour. I didn't show up until the next morning. He could smell the alcohol on my breath. And it wasn't the first time. He absolutely handed my hide to me in that fight. I threw up right after and didn't touch whisky again for almost a decade."

"What were you doing out all night?" I asked. My

stomach knotted at the thought of him with some young crush.

Oh, get over it, Dahlia. He was allowed to have a school-aged girlfriend! He's even allowed to have a girl-friend now. He's his own person.

"Deadwoods," he said. "Me and some of my friends decided to see if we could catch a hidebehind. Dumb idea. You're ten times more likely to be caught by one than you are to catch one. We prowled around, wrestled some hellhounds, made a small fire, and downed a bottle of Sheehan's Small Batch Whisky between the three of us that Shane stole from his dad's liquor cabinet."

"I guess being a teenager is sort of the same everywhere," I said.

"You get into trouble when you were younger, too?" he asked, side-eyeing me with a sly grin.

"Sorry to disappoint, but no. I watched a lot of my classmates get into trouble, though. Drinking, staying out all night. Most of it was harmless and they'd stumble home the next morning and swear off alcohol for a while. Not all of them learned that lesson, but most did."

"You're telling me you haven't yet?"

I considered it. "I haven't learned it the hard way, if that's what you're asking."

"The hard way is the best way," he replied. "Sure, my dad gave me what for, but it was still one of the best nights of my life. Shane and Clive are two of my closest friends to this day."

Shane and Clive, I thought. *Not girls.* I felt a strange sense of relief from that, which was obviously silly.

"I learn best from watching," I said.

"Then you'll learn quite a bit at the clan's solstice

feast, I can tell you that. You'll see things you haven't even imagined. When werebears get together, things can get rowdy. Maybe not at the start of the night, but by the end after a few hours of eating and drinking and having to see family?" He shook his head, grinning.

He was speaking as if I'd already agreed to come, and I decided to neither confirm nor deny that assumption.

As the garden center appeared ahead of us, I paused and looked around. Where was Atlas?

An instant after, he leaped out of a massive snowdrift, sending the powder shooting in all directions.

"*Did you see that?*" he shouted gleefully. "*I could pull off a sneak attack in this stuff!*"

His glee became my glee, and I reached down and made a snowball with my gloved hands. I lobbed it gently at him and he dodged it easily.

"*No one can hit me now!*" he proclaimed before diving back into the snow. He disappeared completely, and my only clue as to his location was the line of displaced snow appearing as he burrowed through the drifts like a groundhog.

"I wish I had this much fun in the snow," said Dante beside me. "I guess I've grown too used to it over the seasons. It's nice to see it fresh through someone else's eyes, though."

I couldn't stop grinning watching Atlas get the snow zoomies out of the blue, even as my lips stayed relatively numb.

I made another snowball and waited. As soon as Atlas jumped out of the snow, I hit him in the side with it. It exploded in a burst of powder, and the adrenaline only accelerated his zoomies. Thankfully we were on the edge of town, and he had plenty of space to run.

He began making large figure eights, and each time he'd get close, Dante and I would lob a few snowballs at him. He was able to dodge most of them. My familiar's joy was contagious, and once I started laughing, I couldn't stop. It made my legs weak, and when my next throw hit Atlas between the eyes, causing him to make the funniest face, I went down, wheezing with laughter. Dante, also in stitches at Atlas's undignified behavior, set the vase out of the way then bent over to lift me up, but Atlas barreled into him. Before we knew it, the three of us were lying in the middle of the cleared path, gasping for air.

I rolled over and petted Atlas on the shoulders, trying to calm him as his eyes remained wide. "You get that out of your system?" I asked.

"I don't know what came over me. Is that what being possessed is?"

"If it is," I replied through our silent connection, *"then may we all be possessed soon."*

Once Dante and I had dusted off the snowflakes from our clothes, with Atlas still panting but otherwise subdued, we walked the rest of the way up the path to Whirligig's.

We passed through the arched gateway of the garden center, Dante holding it open for Atlas and me to pass ahead of him. The place looked like a fairy realm full of massive glistening bubbles. The employees had covered the flowers, no doubt expecting the previous night's snow, to protect the plants. Each transparent half-dome contained an explosion of color beneath it, and even though I couldn't smell the aroma of the blossoms, I could easily imagine it.

"Over there," Dante said, pointing at a small wooden building. "Whoever's working today will be staying warm in there. I'm sure they can grab us a quick bouquet."

He was right about the building being warm. While it was dim inside compared to outside with the sun's reflection off the snow, it was bursting with color. Arrangements of flowers filled shelves that lined the walls, and in the back, sitting at a tall stool and deeply engrossed in a book, was a hulking figure.

He looked up as we entered.

"Uncle Ansel," Dante said, walking over and shaking his hand. "What're you reading?"

Ansel's dark face colored. "Ah, nothing." He tried to slip the book out of sight behind the counter, but Dante snatched it first and held up the cover to read it. "*Wild Magic: Chronicles of Fierce Love*? Since when do you read *this* kind of book?"

Ansel grunted and snatched the book back, stuffing it out of sight. All he said was, "Jane."

Dante's mouth fell open with amusement. "Oh yeah? She has you reading this sort of thing? I didn't even know you read books."

"Why are you here?" Ansel demanded. Dante turned to me, and I felt the embarrassment and annoyance pulsing from the older werebear. And I mean that literally. One of my Fifth Wind talents, it turned out, was feeling what others felt. It seemed that I only experienced it with stronger emotions, especially when the person's emotions were slightly out of control, but there it was. Either his embarrassment was intense or I was growing more sensitive.

Atlas stepped behind me. *"You'd better answer him,"* he said.

"We're here to pick up some flowers for a delivery," I said.

"Fine. Anything specific?"

"Something wintery."

Ansel eyed me suspiciously. Did he think I was being cheeky? "They're all wintery. It's winter. This is what grows."

"Don't be like that," Dante said. "There's the greenhouse for other varieties."

Ansel looked like he might be up for fighting his nephew. "Since you seem to know everything, how about you help her pick out what she needs and let me know when you're ready to pay." He angled his body away from us on the stool, grabbed the book, and began reading again.

I scanned the walls for anything that stuck out to me. All the bouquets were beautiful. It was so amazing that this much color could exist even in wintertime.

Dante sidled up beside me. "Do you have a favorite flower?"

"Not really. That one's pretty, though." I pointed to an indigo blossom that resembled a tiny evergreen tree. "No idea what it's called. Why, do you have a favorite flower?"

"I do actually. I'm a fan of dahlias."

I felt my cheeks heat up and shot a glance at Ansel to see if he'd overheard the obvious flirtation. The roll of his eyes told me he had, but he said nothing and continued to read his romance novel.

Like a stammering fool, I said, "Oh, are dahlias winter flowers?"

"No idea."

Right. Because he probably wasn't talking about the flower.

"He's flirting with you," said Atlas. *"I can smell the pheromones."*

"Thanks for pointing out the obvious," I replied.

"Those will work," I said, stepping forward and pulling a bunch of red and orange flowers from the shelf. "They contrast well with the vase."

"Good call."

As usual, I began second-guessing myself immediately. "Is the red too romantic? We don't actually know who is sending these flowers to whom and for what occasion."

Dante placed a hand on my arm. "If they didn't give us the information, then it's hardly our fault if the colors aren't what they wanted. I think those look great. Whoever they're for should be glad to receive them."

A few minutes later, as we headed out after paying, Dante said, "Give Aunt Jane my love."

Ansel ignored him.

Chapter Three

Dante led us along a path away from the town center once we left Whirligig's behind. "I've never been to Muscoff Manor Inn," he said. "I'm interested to see what it's like."

"But you've clearly heard of it before, or else how would you know where it is?" I replied.

"I only know where it is because we used to creep around it as kids. That was *before* it was an inn. I haven't seen the inside of it other than pressing my face up against the dusty windows."

"It used to be abandoned?" I asked.

"Since before I was born. I only heard about someone renovating it a couple of years ago. It's now marketed as a couple's retreat. Very romantic."

"And you haven't been there before? Not even with—"

He held up a hand to stop me. "Let's not bring her up. And no. Definitely not with her."

"For the record," I said, "I'm fine with you saying her

name. Sure, she tried to murder me, but I don't take it personally."

He arched a brow at me. "Noted. I hope you don't mind if *I* hold a grudge against her for trying to murder you."

"I thought werebears didn't hold grudges."

"We do when we're unable to enter into combat with the person. I wouldn't fight a witch in the first place, but even if I would, I could hardly do it now that she's in Ironhelm Penitentiary for murder." A slight shudder ran through him.

"What's that about?" I asked.

"Nothing."

I pressed my lips together. "Oh, come on. I don't buy that for a second."

Relenting, he said, "I know she did a horrible thing, but... I don't enjoy thinking about her locked away in Ironhelm. It's not a nice place to be."

I placed a gentle hand on his back. "I'm sorry. I don't know much about it, but I can't imagine any penitentiary is a nice place to be. She won't be there forever, though, right?"

"I hope not. She did a horrible thing, but I don't think she's a horrible person. She just sort of lost her mind."

The woods thickened along our path as we reached the base of Fluke Mountain and continued up in a contemplative silence.

"Want me to carry those for a while?" I asked, nodding at the vase. My arms would've been tired carrying it by now, with the flowers and water already in it. But Dante said he was good, and I was inclined to believe him. His biceps weren't massive like a body builder's, but they were clearly all tight, toned cords of muscle. Never considering myself a superficial person, I still found myself thinking about those biceps frequently, even when they were covered by his coat sleeve, as they were then. How had I let him get under my skin like this?

My first glimpse of Muscoff Manor Inn appeared between the trees, and it looked quite lovely, a little like some of the nicer boutique hotels in New Orleans. I'd never been able to stay at one of those, and I doubted Muscoff Manor Inn was any more affordable, but perhaps I'd be able to step inside on the pretense of this delivery to get a quick look around.

The exterior was tan brick with the network of ivy vines climbing up the brick, as could be found on many other buildings in Eastwind. The thick canopy blocked out much of the sun, but warm interior lights glowed through sheer curtains. Even though the building itself was huge, it seemed cozy from where I stood looking at it.

"Certainly doesn't look like the rundown place I used to visit as a kid," said Dante.

We approached the red front door, on which hung a large and richly scented pine wreath, and I knocked as Dante continued holding the flower vase. A moment later, the door swung open, and I was treated to a wave of warmth from inside.

A petite woman with a salt-and-pepper bob and ice-blue eyes behind thick-rimmed spectacles grinned at us from across the threshold. She quickly waved us in. "Come, come! It's too cold outside."

I stepped inside, followed by Dante, but when the woman saw Atlas, she sucked in air. "Sorry. No pets allowed."

I was momentarily confused, considering a scrawny gray tabby had just appeared at her ankles, its back arched at the new arrivals.

"Oh, um..."

"*Not a problem,*" Atlas said. "*I'd rather stay out here than be cooped up in a strange building.*"

"*I hope you don't feel rejected,*" I said.

"*I do, but I'm used to it. I'd rather be safe than included.*"

Poor, sweet Atlas. The boldness from his zoomies had clearly worn off. I made a mental note to give him a pep talk before bed tonight.

Atlas disappeared into the nearest snow drift, and the petite woman shut the door behind us. "Welcome, welcome! I'm Gloriana Drawforth, the innkeeper. At your service for the duration of your stay. May I have the name under which you reserved your room?"

"Oh. We're not guests," I clarified hastily.

She looked at Dante and me, a deep line appearing between her brows, then she blinked, and her smile returned. "Ah, I assumed you were one of our couples. That's my mistake."

"We're here on a delivery," I said, and Dante held up the flowers.

"Phew! I didn't remember there being any other reservations for the day that hadn't already checked in. For a moment there, I was concerned I might've accidentally double-booked a room."

The tabby slinked in a figure eight around Gloriana's ankles. Then I heard it say, "*I don't like them. Especially the big one. Werebears are dumb brutes.*"

Ah, a familiar, then. Which meant Gloriana Draw-forth was a witch.

I made it a point not to let anyone know that I could listen in on the telepathic communication of other witches' familiars. For one, it seemed like the rudest power imaginable, and I didn't want to pry, even if that's what ended up happening. But for another, hearing what familiars had to say when they didn't know anyone but their witch was listening could be useful, especially if the witch was hiding something that only her familiar knew.

I had no reason to believe that was the case with Gloriana and her tabby, though. The older witch seemed quite congenial.

"And who are the flowers for?" she asked.

"We're not sure," I said. "I was only given the address and room."

"Quite strange," she replied. "But stranger things have happened here. I suppose it's part of some romantic surprise. We're a couple's retreat, you know. Romance is mysterious, if nothing else."

A large portrait on the wall that stared down at us caught my attention. The figure had a fair, oval face and dark, piercing eyes. His black hair ran down his shoulders, and the small points at the top of his ears stuck out between the curtains of his hair. He was wearing a formal tunic with ruffles around the collar and a navy-blue coat.

"Ah," said Gloriana. "I see you've noticed our guardian. Linton Muscoff. The original owner of Muscoff Manor. He lived here for many years before passing. An elf from Avalon. The story goes that he made a fortune off the gem mines in Avalon and decided he was done with the demands of city life... and people in general. He bought land out here, back when Fluke Mountain was still mostly unsettled, commissioned the building of his manor, and was never seen again. Had everything he needed delivered to his doorstep, and only took it inside once the courier had left."

There was a time in my life where I was likely headed on a similar path toward hermitage, though not necessarily willingly. Thank goodness I died before that could happen.

"Sounds lonely," I said, staring at Muscoff's stern expression in the portrait.

"Some might feel that way. He certainly didn't. He lived alone for two hundred years before it's estimated that he passed."

"And how does anyone know when he died, if he lived alone and never saw anyone?" Dante asked.

Gloriana shrugged. "Presumably Ted paid him a visit. The reaper has his ways of knowing when someone's passed, hasn't he?"

"Makes sense," said Dante.

Gloriana narrowed her eyes at me. "*You* might know more about Ted's brand of skills than most. You're the new Fifth Wind witch in town, aren't you?"

"That's me. Dahlia Wildes."

"Hm," was all she said. Her tabby did the talking when he arched his back and hissed.

"Now, now, Givens," she said. "We don't practice prejudice here. Dahlia seems like a lovely person." She returned her attention to me. "I'm quite friendly with Ruby True, you know. We're both regulars at A New Leaf since it reopened. I have no problem with Fifth Winds."

"Thanks," I said, because what else was there to say? Was I supposed to feel grateful that she didn't hate me for something I couldn't control? Not being biased about things people couldn't control felt like the bare minimum of being a good person. But I also knew from experience when people started that they didn't hate you for who you were, they were usually looking for a little gratitude in return. I'd certainly encountered the same thing back in New Orleans from time to time, though it was with regards to my darker skin color, not any magical powers.

A wave of hostility hit me, and I turned toward the source. Dante was glaring at Gloriana, his jaw visibly clenched. Oh boy. Clearly, he couldn't blow off her attitude the same way I could. Time to get a move on. "Room D," I said. "That's where these are supposed to be delivered."

"Of course! I almost forgot about the flowers." Gloriana pointed us toward the open staircase at the opposite end of the entry hall. "Up and to your left. The doors have the letters nailed on them, so you won't miss it. I'll be in the kitchen, brewing tea for the guests if you need me. Just through there." She pointed through what appeared to be a dining room just off the entry. A door leading off it must've been where she meant. "But I don't expect you'll have any issues finding the room. Come Givens." The cat prowled away but checked over his shoulder multiple times to meow aggressively at us.

Once she was out of earshot, Dante grumbled, "She has a lot of nerve keeping Atlas out while that furball stalks around. Either you allow familiars in or you don't."

"In her defense," I said, "she probably didn't want Atlas tracking in a bunch of mud and snow. My guess is that she's in charge of keeping the place clean." My mind flashed through a few specific scenarios from my house-cleaner days where I'd just finished mopping a floor and the homeowner's children came barreling through without even removing their shoes. Not fun.

We made for the stairs. "I just don't like her," he muttered. "The tone she used when talking about having a friend who's a Fifth Wind..."

"I know," I said. "I'm familiar with the tone."

"They see each other at a tea shop? That's hardly friends."

"I know," I repeated, though I didn't mind him airing the grievances. I felt them, too, but putting them to words was never my strong suit.

As we climbed the stairs, the fierce eyes of Linton Muscoff seemed to follow us from the portrait's frame, and the air around me felt thick. It was an oppressive feeling that started as pressure against my skin but began to seep inside of me. I couldn't describe it, but I felt my mood shift. Perhaps it was the come down from tolerating Gloriana's subtle aspersions. I should've stood up to her about Atlas, maybe even called her out about her thin attempt to prove she wasn't prejudiced against Fifth Winds. But I hadn't. I never did. I was weak in that regard. Meek. I couldn't even get properly annoyed about it like Dante could. I probably deserved it if I was going to sit there in silence the whole time...

"It's not a terrible place," Dante said, taking in the freshly wallpapered hallway. "I wouldn't mind staying here." He cast me a sideways glance, and I remembered Gloriana's initial mistake of believing Dante and I were a couple. She must really be getting old if she thought he and I could not only be together but would be in a serious enough relationship to come to a place like this. Instead, our relationship felt stuck in a liminal space. He'd expressed his attraction to me, and I'd confirmed my feelings in my own way, but we weren't yet together. And that was probably for the best. He would eventually realize I wasn't worth the time and effort of dating. It was better to keep him at arm's length until he discovered that than have him figure it out once we were already in something committed. The last thing I wanted was for him to feel trapped with me.

"What's up?" he said as we reached the top of the stairs. He gazed down at me over the flower arrangement in his arms.

"What do you mean?"

"You're really silent. And not a peaceful silence."

"I'm fine," I lied. I certainly wasn't feeling great in the moment, but my mood seemed justified.

"I don't believe you. Is it the... I can't describe it, but this place feels stuffy all of a sudden. Is it that?"

"Stuffy?" That was sort of what I'd felt come over me, but I wouldn't have described it that way. Was my mood related to the stuffiness?

An eruption of raised voices disrupted my thoughts. The shouting grew louder as we walked down the hallway, passing room A on our left.

"You hear that?" Dante asked. I nodded.

Once we reached room D, it was clear that the shouting was coming from inside.

"It's like I'm invisible to you!" came a woman's voice. "Like you don't even see me at all! Would it kill you to give me your undivided attention for *once*?"

Then a man's voice replied, "You think I don't? If I gave you all the attention you seem to need, I wouldn't have attention left for anything else! I've tried to give you what you need, Haven, and it was never good enough! When I give you attention, all you want is more! You're sucking me dry!"

"I'm not asking too much," she snapped. "You simply don't have enough to give!"

Dante and I exchanged glances, both of us cringing.

He whispered, "Maybe I should just..." and nodded at the small rug in front of the door for Room D.

"Sounds smart."

He placed the vase on the floor just to the side of the door so that it would be visible but not likely to be knocked over by, say, anyone storming out of the room. Then he jabbed a thumb toward the way out, and I giggled nervously and silently as we quickly tiptoed away from the argument.

Once we were down the stairs and heading for the front door, we passed a parlor on our right, where I spotted two men who appeared to be in their late forties, one with fair skin and silver-blond hair, the other much darker in both complexion and hair. They sat across a small table from each other, drinking tea in complete silence. Whether they were there earlier or had just come down for the tea Gloriana brewed for them, I wasn't sure, but what I did know was that a wave of resentment rolled out of that room and hit me square on. My hands balled into fists, even though I could tell that the emotion wasn't mine. Strange.

Some couples' retreat, I thought, forcing my hands to unclench.

It was a relief to step outside again, even if that meant going back into the cold. I shivered and pulled my coat tighter around me.

"It's nice to be back outside," Dante remarked.

"I agree."

"Did you see that couple in the parlor?" he asked.

"I did."

"Probably good that they're spending time at a couples' retreat. They didn't seem too happy with each other."

I clenched and unclenched my fingers until I felt the last drips of animosity leave them. "You can say that again."

To my surprise, Dante offered me his arm. I looked down at it then up into his face. "Are you serious?"

"Of course. The sun is melting the snow. It could get slippery out here."

"Such a gentleman," I teased. "Worried about me falling and injuring myself?"

"You?" he said, his brows arching. "Who said anything about you? I'm hoping you'll keep *me* from falling. I'm much larger than you. It'll hurt more for me to bust my hide."

I laughed and took the arm he offered. The negative thoughts I'd had about myself in the house earlier felt distant and foreign. Why not enjoy my time with Dante when it was naturally so enjoyable? I deserved that much, even if it might never turn to something more serious.

Atlas appeared from a drift, shaking out the snow from his fur before loping up to us.

"Have a nice rest?" I asked him.

"Not at all. A fox snuck up on me and tried to attack."

"A fox?" I responded silently. I didn't want to embarrass him in front of Dante. *"And how do you know it was trying to attack you?"* I couldn't imagine any fox in its right mind trying to take on a hellhound ten times its size.

"I can just tell. She was hopping into the drifts, looking for a victim."

"A victim like a mouse?"

"Or a hellhound with his guard down."

I sighed, recognizing a conversation to nowhere when I saw it, and settled for giving Atlas a reassuring scratch behind the ears.

We paused where the road leading away from Muscoff Manor Inn split, and Dante said, "I'm heading home for lunch. Been eating out too much, and I'll probably end up at Franco's for dinner anyway, since I get the employee discount there. Want to join? I'm thinking of putting together a stew for lunch."

That did sound delicious. And then I imagined being alone with Dante in his home, and my stomach twisted into a knot. "Rain check? I should check in with Sasha and see if she needs a break before my shift starts later."

He didn't seem offended. Instead, he turned to face me head-on, staring down into my eyes. "Okay. I'd love to cook for you sometime soon, though."

There was almost no air between our bodies, and I felt heat from him that seemed more than a simple result of temperature.

He bowed his head slightly, and I held my breath. My heart raced, and adrenaline surged through my arms. He ran a large palm down one, and time seemed to stop. The world around us disappeared, and I felt a split urge to both run away and stand my ground. Should I close my eyes? That was usually how this was done. But I couldn't stop staring at him. It was a struggle not to stare directly at his lips, anticipating what they would feel like.

And then he pulled back. "Watch your step as you walk downhill. I'd hate for you to take a bad fall."

I let out the breath I was holding. "Right. Yes. I'll keep a hand on Atlas."

His eyes flickered down me, and then he turned and headed toward his home.

I stood there like a dummy, staring after him.

Had he been waiting for me to make the first move? Why would he do that? Or had the thought of kissing me never even crossed his mind?

"I should've made the move," I lamented.

"No. You were being smart."

"I certainly don't feel smart."

"Kissing is a vulnerable position. When you close your eyes and let your guard down, that's when you're most vulnerable to an attack!"

"Thanks for the wisdom, Atlas." And then we wandered back toward town.

Chapter Four

"*Something about you is off*," said Atlas as we entered Eastwind proper. "*It's making me nervous.*"

He was certainly perceptive. While my head felt much clearer having left the manor, I didn't feel completely rid of it. "Something was strange about that place. I can't put my finger on it exactly, but I keep thinking about it. It was a couples' retreat, but no one seemed happy there. Even me. I felt like rubbish about myself. But maybe that's just an old habit. I've never been accused of having a big head about myself."

"*Sounds scary.*"

"I wouldn't necessarily say that. Tense, more like. Odd. The room where we were supposed to deliver the flowers? There was a couple inside it, yelling. It sounded like quite the argument."

"*I'm glad I stayed outside then. I hate the sound of yelling. It reminds me of the way my bullies used to howl in the Deadwoods when they would chase me.*"

I moved closer to him and pressed his head up against my side. "You're safe now."

"Safer, maybe. But never completely safe."

My stomach growled. I hadn't turned down Dante's offer because I wasn't hungry, after all.

Atlas heard the growl as his head pressed into my side. *"I would risk my safety for a plate of meatballs,"* he said.

"I don't think we should go to Dante's work when I already told him I'd be heading to Time to Kiln." I sighed. "What a stupid lie. And now I have to spend this energy covering for it. So pointless. I wish I'd just said yes." But then I imagined being alone at Dante's house with him, and my empty stomach turned into a knot. "What about the place with the dumplings?" I said. "We've been meaning to try that, and I finally have money of my own to spend on it."

Atlas was willing to brave a new environment for dumplings. Who wouldn't be? Hot dumplings on a cold day? Not much was better than that.

The restaurant was warm, and the dumplings were even better than I'd expected. Worth the look of surprise I got from the host when I walked in with a hellhound by my side. She sat us right away, and I felt much, much better once I had some food in me. Atlas seemed slightly calmer by the end of the meal, too.

My shift at Time to Kiln didn't start for another hour, but I had nothing better to do than head that way.

I pushed open the door of the shop, the bell tinkling as I did, and saw a tall figure in a gray trench coat with her back to me. She was chatting with Sasha, who leaned to the side to look at me as I entered.

Nora Ashcroft turned around. "Oh good! There you are. I was looking for you."

"You were?" I tried to think of all the reasons she might want to speak to me that couldn't have waited until I was back at her house later that evening. Was this something about the winter solstice? Was she going to invite me to something? Or perhaps tell me she and Tanner had other plans that I wasn't invited to?

It was none of those things.

"I could use your help," she said. "There's been a murder. Tanner and Stu are stuck on calls at the moment, and Sheriff Bloom is apparently out of the office on vacation. I could probably handle it on my own, but I'd rather not. Plus, you catch things I don't." I appreciated her being discrete about my ability to feel the emotions of others. It was privileged information, and I didn't know how Sasha would feel about it or if I could trust her to keep it quiet.

"Another murder?" I asked. What I didn't say but referred to was that there had been a murder only a few weeks before, and this seemed like a high rate for such a small town.

Nora seemed to understand my question, because she said, "Yes, it's the friendliest dangerous small town you'll ever visit. And to be fair, I don't know that it's a murder yet. The report via emergency owl said it was, but it's probably best not to jump to conclusions. People don't usually make the most sense after finding a dead body."

I turned to Sasha, and before I could open my mouth, the elf rolled her eyes. "Sure, I'll cover for you for a few hours. Then I'll close early. Jude and Raven will understand. No one's shopping in this weather anyway."

"Thank you."

Nora shot me a thumbs up. "Ready?"

"As ready as I'll ever be for murder. Where are we headed?"

Despite all the strange things that happened in this town, her answer was the last thing I expected.

"It's a little ways out of town. It happened at a place called Muscoff Manor Inn."

Chapter Five

"What's wrong?" Nora asked, inspecting my expression closely.

I tried to speak, but too many thoughts swirled in my mind.

Sasha was kind enough to answer. "She was just up there this morning. A flower delivery."

"Really?" asked Nora, squinting harder at me.

"Yes. But I didn't see any dead bodies while I was there," I managed to reply.

"Then it must've happened after you left." She paused, chewing on her bottom lip. "Definitely strange." Buttoning up her coat, she strode toward the door of the shop. "We'll just have to find out what's going on."

When we stepped outside, I spotted Grim, Nora's big black familiar, with his leg raised, creating a large amount of yellow snow by the corner of the pottery shop. A second later, my eyes caught movement in the snow next to a nearby tree, and I found Atlas occupied with the same craft, if you could call it that.

"Oh look," said Nora, "a literal pissing contest."

I giggled into my palm. "Atlas, whenever you're done there, we're heading back to Muscoff Manor."

"Maybe you are," he replied. *"I'm not. That place gave me the creeps."*

"And where are you going instead?" I asked.

"He's coming with me," said Grim.

"And where are *you* going?" Nora asked.

"Where do you think? Medium Rare."

Nora and I looked at each other. "At least they'll be out of trouble," she said.

"Atlas really didn't like the inn. I can hardly ask him to come with me again. It's not like I'll be in danger, right?"

Nora shrugged. "None that we can't get ourselves out of."

And so, we allowed the hellhounds to ditch the investigation, not that we could've told them what to do anyhow.

While I liked having Atlas by my side (even if he was scared of the world, the world didn't know that), it warmed my heart to watch his big, shaggy white butt trotting away next to Grim's big, shaggy black butt. I was so glad Atlas had a hellhound friend. He deserved one.

Nora and I started toward Fluke Mountain. "It probably goes without saying," she began, "that you're a person of interest in this case."

"Really?" I asked, shocked.

She suppressed a smile. "Sure. You were at the inn right around the time of the murder. That puts you on the list. But don't worry"—she nudged me with her elbow — "I'm pretty sure I can cross you off quickly. Were you alone in the house for the delivery, or was Atlas with you?"

"Atlas stayed outside, but Dante was with me."

"See? You already have someone to corroborate your story, so you'll be free and clear in no time."

I couldn't tell if she was giving me a hard time or not. "You think I could murder someone?"

"Definitely," she said cheerily. "Anyone could. I don't think you would murder someone on purpose, though."

"And why's that?" I asked.

"Just a hunch from having spent so much time together, but I don't think you have a mean bone in your body. That being said, our powers can be fickle things. I know as I was discovering the full extent of mine, I did a few things I wish I hadn't, got in over my head once or twice. Or fifty times. *If* you had anything to do with the murder, I would assume it wasn't intentional."

"Sheesh..." I stared down at my boots as they crunched over the snow. "Now you have me suspecting myself."

"For what it's worth, we'll know a lot more once we get to the inn. I don't even know who the victim is yet."

She had a point. Could the deceased be someone Dante and I had seen in our brief visit there? Or one of the other guests?

"I hope it's not the innkeeper," I said. "She was very welcoming."

"Welcoming? What do you mean? I assumed you dropped the flowers off and left."

"No, we went inside to drop them at the specific room. She mistook Dante and I for guests when we first arrived."

I proceeded to fill her in on the short visit, including the relevant information, which seemed only to be that the couple was arguing, so we left the flowers at the door and headed out.

Those were the facts that I knew, but there were so many other parts of that visit that stuck out to me. I didn't see how they were relevant, though, and telling her about the crabby tabby or the unflattering thoughts I had might make me seem paranoid. It all felt relevant, sure, but I didn't know how, so I could hardly explain it.

When we knocked on the front door to Muscoff Manor Inn, Gloriana swung open the door, a finger already pressed to her lips. "I'm trying to keep the fuss to a minimum to avoid disturbing the other guests," she said, and then she waved us inside.

I felt such relief in discovering that she hadn't been murdered that I nodded compliantly and didn't speak. Next to me, Nora seemed to bristle at the directive, but she didn't go out of her way to make noise.

Gloriana took our jackets, hanging them by the door as Givens arched his back at us. She hadn't offered that service when Dante and I arrived with the delivery, but this would likely be a longer visit.

Nora stomped the snow off her boots onto the rug, asking, "Where is the body?"

"Upstairs," Gloriana replied hardly above a whisper. "I'll show you. And if there's any possibility we could get this cleaned up and out of the way before the guests come down for supper, that would be greatly appreciated."

"That's up to Ted and the deputies," Nora explained. "We're just here in the meantime to see what we can learn about it."

Gloriana's anxiety was palpable. "But you and Ted are close, are you not? Maybe you can call in a favor to have him come as soon as possible."

"Sorry," Nora replied. "Death works on Death's time."

As we headed toward the stairs at the back of the entryway, I caught a glimpse into the parlor. The two witches who had looked so tense earlier were still in there, but now they were joined by a third man, presumably an elf by the look of him, who was hunched over, his head in his hands. The witches sat on either side of him, providing comfort with hands on his back and soothing, whispered words.

I was not totally surprised when Gloriana led us to Room D. My foresight had paid off, and the vase of flowers still sat to the side of the door, undisturbed by the death that had happened so nearby. Not that it mattered since the intended recipient wasn't around to enjoy them.

The victim was lying flat on her back, just inside the door. Her eyes were still open as she stared blankly at the ceiling.

"That's her," said Gloriana.

"Oh, come on," said Nora exasperatedly, kneeling immediately beside the victim's head to close her eyes. She glared over her shoulder at the innkeeper, who she clearly believed should've already handled this basic dignity.

"I'm sorry," Gloriana replied. "Seeing her gave me such a start, I left the room as fast as I could to send the emergency owl to the Sheriff's Department. I've never seen a dead body before."

Gloriana clutched at a small charm on her necklace,

keeping both of her hands close to her chest. I wouldn't have been particularly shocked to see her fall down and curl into a fetal position.

I could hardly blame her. This was only the second dead body I'd encountered, and it was hard to look at.

Givens slinked into the room, rubbed around his witch's legs, then approached the body with curiosity. *"She would've hated to see herself this way. Very unflattering for an elf as vain as she was."*

"Givens," Gloriana snipped. "Stay away from the body! This is a crime scene, for fang's sake."

"Presumably this is a guest?" Nora asked, her eyes still on the victim's face as she stood.

"Yes. She was staying in this room. Her name is Haven Featherbreeze, and from what she told me, she and her husband are on a vacation from Avalon."

Nora's brows shot up. "Avalonian elves came *here* for a vacation?"

I didn't know much about Avalon, though I'd gleaned some things about it from overheard conversations. It appeared to be a whole other realm, but one connected by train to Eastwind. I suspected it was more cosmopolitan, too. In the snippets I'd overheard from Eastwinders, there was a subtle hostility toward those from Avalon that came through, and I sensed that same bit of hostility from Nora now. It was the kind that colored the voices of those in New Orleans when they talked about investors coming to buy up property for vacation rentals.

Gloriana puffed up her chest. "It wouldn't be the first time Avalonians made Muscoff Manor Inn their vacation destination of choice. We offer high-end service, all meals included, and I've heard it's a nice break from the hustle and bustle of city life."

"Fair enough," Nora said, clearly disinterested in the sales pitch. "And where is her husband?"

I jumped in. "He's downstairs in the parlor, isn't he? That's him I saw?"

Gloriana bowed her head. "Yes, his name is Astaire Ripple. I'm afraid he's terribly upset. He was the one to find her."

"We'll need to speak with him," Nora replied.

"Of course," said the innkeeper. "I'll bring him up."

When she returned a moment later with Astaire, his fair elfin face was beet red, but there was no swelling around his eyes to indicate he'd been crying. He was visibly distraught, however, and I reminded myself that everyone reacted differently to traumatic and life-changing moments. Some people went numb, some became hysterical, and some experienced a clarity of mind that left them feeling strangely calm. There was no right way to discover your wife dead, so there was no wrong way, either.

Unless you were the one who murdered her, I thought morbidly.

"As difficult as it is, Mr. Ripple," said Nora, "please don't touch or move her. Have you already moved her, or is this how you found her?"

His response was unhelpful. "Haven! My dear, sweet Haven! I never meant those things I said to you! I'd do anything to take it back! Anything!"

It was his voice I'd heard behind the door when I'd delivered the flowers, then. He and his wife, the victim, were the ones arguing. I took a deep breath and tried to sense what emotion dominated his words.

Guilt. Deep guilt. But about what? From his final words to her being said out of anger or from something much more sinister?

I was standing just inside Room D, keeping out of the way, which was my forte, when another figure appeared in the doorway.

It was impossible not to take a step back when I looked at her full on. Her presence was that powerful. Despite the thick, fuzzy robe and slippers she wore, there was a radiance about her that occupied physical space. The moment she appeared in the doorway, it felt like she was in charge.

"What in Heaven's name?" she said.

All eyes in the room turned toward her, and Nora was the first to speak. "Sheriff Bloom? What...?" Her words broke off as she took in the woman's outfit.

Ah, so this was the sheriff I'd heard so much about. No wonder. She commanded attention even in her most cozy clothes. It was partly the assertive presence, but I didn't discount the effect of her height. If Bloom wasn't six feet tall, I'd eat my own fist.

She stepped forward, entering the room, and that's when I saw that her robe had two slits in the back, through which massive white wings poked but rested flat against her back.

"I'm terribly sorry," Gloriana said, rushing forward to intercept the sheriff. "I promised not to disturb you on your vacation, and here you are, standing over a dead body. But I'm already taking care of it. It's being properly handled, so you are free to return to your—"

"When did this happen?" the sheriff asked, addressing Nora.

"Not sure yet, still getting preliminary information."

Even Astaire's grief had folded under the sheriff's sudden presence, and he stared dumbly at her.

"Astaire," said Bloom, "I think it's in your best interest if you leave the room until we're ready to—" She snapped her eyes and mouth closed, cutting herself off. "Nope." Holding up her hands, she said, "Nora, it's all yours. I'm on vacation. Old habits. I trust Culpepper or Manchester are on their way?"

Nora shot her a thumbs up. "We're on it."

"Wonderful. And if you need me for any of this... don't." She turned on her heel and walked out of the room. The sense of calm command left along with her.

"The sheriff is right," Nora said. "Astaire, I think we'd better take you somewhere else to talk." She paused. "I'll stay here and update Tanner or Stu when they arrive. Dahlia, maybe you and Astaire can head out."

I felt the blood leave my face. "Me?"

Nora nodded.

I hurried over to her, whispering, "What do you want me to ask him about exactly?"

"What happened. Get a timeline from him. See what he knows."

"Right," I said, rolling my shoulders back, as if that would cure my anxiety.

Fake it till you make it did not work in this case. I was still worried about messing this up. But Astaire and I followed Gloriana out of Room D and into a small study across the hall anyway. Ready or not, I was in charge of interviewing our prime suspect.

Chapter Six

The cozy study had two small chairs by a fireplace, a writing desk in the corner, and packed bookshelves around walls. Beside the chairs were two small tables, each hardly large enough to hold a tea saucer. There was no fire burning when I entered and the only light came from multi-wick candles burning in two large sconces on either side of the mantle. Astaire gazed fixedly ahead at one of them, the light casting dark, darting shadows on his face.

I was prepared to work with the lighting we had until the innkeeper waved her wand at the fireplace and the logs burst into flame. "I'll fetch some herbal tea," she said, leaving Astaire and me alone together.

This felt like a lot of responsibility, but I reminded myself that I had done an investigation like this before, more or less. What would Nora do? That seemed like a reasonable guiding question.

"Astaire, can you tell me about your day so far?"

"It's been jolly good. No complaints. Hardly memorable at all."

I bit my tongue, not appreciating the sarcasm, but also accepting that I could have phrased that better. "I mean the order of events starting from when you woke up until you learned what happened to your wife."

He hugged himself tightly as he slumped back in the chair. He fixed his attention now on the patterned rug in front of the hearth. "I—I woke up. We woke up. Haven and me. Before sunrise. We're early risers." He swallowed hard, perhaps remembering that she would not be rising again any time soon (at least I hoped not for all our sakes). "She did her usual primping, and I read my book. It's a history of early Avalonian architecture. I'm an architect." He shook his head. "No, of course you don't care about that. I hardly care about that after doing it for so long. We went down to breakfast once it was served, and it was just another day. We'd had a bit of a row the night before—we've been doing that a lot lately, I'm afraid. She says... It doesn't matter now, I suppose. I would argue with her every day of my life if it meant having her back. None of her nagging seems unpleasant now. I would do anything to get it back, to have her nag me even one more time." And finally, Astaire burst into tears.

His grief was overwhelming to be near. It swirled around me, and I found myself coughing after a deep inhale of it. It was that thick around me.

We seemed to be in the moment where it finally hit him what he'd lost. I'd never experienced that myself. My parents and siblings all outlived me when I was in New Orleans, and I never lost anyone close to me. Yet I could feel what he was going through with my new powers, and it was excruciating. I almost started crying along with him.

Not now, Dahlia. Leave him space for his own grieving. Let it be his. You have an investigation to run.

The thought of Nora walking in only to find me sobbing with Astaire and no progress made on the basics of his daily movements was enough to bring me to my senses.

His grief seemed very real, though when I dug deeper into it there was a great well of regret buried in it. Someone could surely murder someone, regret it, and then grieve the loss, right? It wasn't impossible. People made mistakes, let their emotions get the best of them all the time.

I fought the urge to get out of my chair and comfort him. For one, that didn't seem very professional, since he was a suspect. But then, I did this thing I always do and accidentally overthought it. Now I couldn't imagine a way of doing it that wasn't physically awkward. Did I kneel next to his chair? Bend over him and give him a hug?

I opted for a simple, "I'm sorry, Astaire. This is an awful moment."

He sniffled and slowly pulled himself together. "I want to assist in any way I can. I'm fine. You can keep asking me questions if it helps find out what happened to her."

My fingertips itched to pet Atlas as he went on. "We were fine this morning. The argument had blown over. Haven and I were together for nearly fifty years, so last night was not exactly our first disagreement."

I quickly tried to do the mental math, since Astaire

hardly looked fifty himself, but then I let it drop. I didn't know much about elves in general. Sasha Cosmo at Time to Kiln was friendly, but she wasn't one to teach the ways of her people without anyone asking directly about it.

"Did anything suspicious happen at breakfast?" I asked. "Any animosity that you observed between Haven and the other guests?"

Gosh, I sounded like a real investigator, didn't I?

"It was a silent breakfast; I did note that. We checked in yesterday afternoon, as did the other guests, and the spirit was much livelier at dinner. Perhaps the wine had something to do it, but I felt like there was much more chatter even prior to the wine being poured. The silence this morning felt... tense. Mostly. Florian and Nestor weren't speaking to one another, when they'd been quite affectionate with each other the night before."

"Florian and Nestor?" I asked. "Other guests?"

"Yes. A pair of witches. They're local to Eastwind, apparently, but they said they don't go out much. Nestor owns a store for witch attire, and Florian works in the kitchen at Hagseed Café. Very lovely people, though. Haven and I got on quite well with them last night. I hadn't been expecting it, frankly. I usually have little in common with witches."

"Who else was at breakfast this morning?" I asked.

"There was Gabby."

"Gabby?"

"Yes, the angel."

"Oh!" I said. "You mean Sheriff Bloom."

He nodded slowly. "Yes, I suppose so. She didn't mention anything about it last night, though. Just introduced herself as Gabby Bloom."

"She's on vacation," I explained. "Was she quiet this morning as well?"

"She was, but she was also reserved last night. This morning, she was reading a book at the table. She didn't even seem to notice that the rest of us were silent."

"And that was it? Just the five guests? You, Haven, Gabby, Florian, and Nestor?"

"That's who was seated, yes. Then Gloriana and Wayne served us. Oh, and that awful tabby lingered around." He shuddered. "I thought familiars were supposed to be warm, but that one... the opposite."

"Wayne?" I asked.

Astaire shrugged. "He's the kitchen help or something. I don't know. Strange fellow. Gave Haven the creeps."

"Why's that?"

"One of those overly helpful people. Doesn't say much but pushes food and trips over himself to make sure everyone's cup is full. A servant to the bones. Hard to respect one of those."

That just sounded like good hospitality to me, but maybe the expectations in Avalon were different from the American South.

"Anything else you noticed about breakfast?" I asked. I was really grasping for something, anything to send me in one direction or another. So far, I felt like I had nothing.

"Besides the eggs being slightly overcooked? Not really. Haven and I left the table as soon as we were finished. Gloriana refilled our teacups, and we headed upstairs to read and relax."

"How long after you returned to your room did you and Haven start arguing?"

His eyes almost crossed at the question. "Who told you we were arguing?"

Did I mention that nobody had told me? That I'd overheard it on my own? I considered it. After all, defaulting to the truth was usually best. But it would likely get us way off track, too. Why was I delivering flowers? If I worked at Time to Kiln, what was I doing interviewing him? His emotional distress had clearly worked to my benefit so far, in that he hadn't stopped to wonder why I was the person asking all these questions. Best not to start him down that path of asking *me* the questions.

"Don't worry how I know. I know. When did the argument between you and Haven start, Mr. Ripple?"

I tried not to grin at how serious I sounded, switching to his last name. I might not have been a real detective, but I could've played one on TV!

"It wasn't long after returning to our room. I settled in with my book and tea, and she started in on me."

"Started in on you? About what?"

He sighed heavily. "She seemed to have some big hopes for this trip. You must understand that after fifty years together, there's not that much left to talk about. My attention has never strayed to other people—that is to say, I've never been disloyal to our vows—and it was easy for me to keep it that way. I don't notice other people all that often. I never have. I'd much rather think about *things*. About concepts. Logical problems. Innovative architectural ideas. But Haven always wants to talk about feelings. Particularly her feelings."

He didn't appear to notice his use of the present

tense when talking about her, and I didn't bother correcting him. His mind would have plenty of time to catch up later.

"We fell into a routine together in Avalon," he continued. "Work, come home, prepare dinner together, enjoy it, read books, go to sleep. I was quite happy with it, but apparently it was slowly tearing her to pieces. I had no idea until she told me. Like I said, I was happy with the routine. I don't always enjoy my work, but I look forward to coming home each night, cooking with my wife, and then settling down with a book. It suits me. But it didn't suit her, and that's why she planned this retreat. She wanted us to get out of the routine and reconnect. I don't know what she meant by that. Reconnect? What does that even mean. We've been together for fifty years. I've been loyal to her that whole time. We share— *shared* a house and meals and an account at the bank. How were we not already connected? That's what last night's argument was about. She was upset that I was reading after dinner like I usually do and tore into me about neglecting her. So, I put the book away and gave her as much attention as I could. Unfortunately, when she started talking, I didn't find any of it interesting. Maybe that's wrong of me to admit. I enjoyed Haven's presence very much. Her thoughts and interests, however... I found most of them shallow and vapid. I don't care who is dating who in the upper echelon on Avalon. I don't care what scandals are erupting. I enjoy doing things with Haven, but it's been a long, long time since I enjoyed our conversations. She never enjoyed the things I wanted to discuss either. We simply had nothing to talk about. I was content with that reality, but she was not."

Gloriana returned with the tea and clearly wanted to hang around and listen in, but I thanked her and waited until she took the hint and left before continuing the conversation with Astaire. "Was that also what the two of you were fighting about this afternoon?" I asked. "Your reading habit?"

"Unfortunately, yes," he said. "I knew it irked her, but I was still annoyed from the argument last night and... maybe I was looking to antagonize her. I don't know. I didn't see it that way at the time." He shook his head miserably. "Bickering. What a stupid way to spend your last conversation with the person you love."

His story matched up from what I'd overheard of the argument. She wasn't getting the attention she wanted from her husband, and he wasn't interested in giving her attention in that way.

I wanted to tell him that he couldn't've known it was his last conversation with her, but that was to be determined. If he'd been the one to kill her, then he *had* known.

However, the prevailing emotions I was getting off him now were the same as before: grief and regret.

"What happened after the argument?" I asked.

"There wasn't really an 'after the argument.' I grew fed up with talking in circles, so I grabbed my book and left. She needed to cool down. We both did. I went downstairs to the parlor, where I found Florian and Nestor. They were kind enough to help me calm my nerves and get my head on straight. I felt much better after my conversation with them. I even considered going upstairs and apologizing, promising to do better for her because at the end of the day, I loved her, and so maybe I ought to work to better care about the things she cared about, even if I found them dull and unfulfilling. Maybe I could challenge myself to better understand what aspects of human affairs interested her. But it was too late."

"What do you mean?" I asked. I sipped a fresh cup of fragrant herbal tea. It was both calming and delicious. *Eastwind might just convert me from coffee to tea before long,* I thought.

"I mean it was too late to change my ways with her because she was already dead." He gasped at having said it and then hurriedly reached for his cup of tea.

I allowed him a moment to benefit from the warm comfort of it then said, "Can you walk me through how you found out? Step-by-step, if you could."

The procedural response seemed to give him something to focus on, and his brow furrowed as he focused his gaze like a laser beam on the surface of his drink. "I was downstairs, speaking with the witches in the parlor. They were comforting me quite effectively, although I admit I was being difficult. It took a lot of conversation before my hard feelings toward Haven began to soften. Perhaps even half an hour, though I wasn't watching the clock. Then Florian stepped out of the room—I'd assumed he needed to use the facilities. It couldn't have been three minutes later that he came running back into the parlor, his face white as a ghost. He pulled Nestor into the entryway to speak, and then the two returned and told me that Florian had just found... he'd just discovered Haven upstairs. Dead." He seemed to remember he was holding a drink and took a small sip. "I was stunned, confused. It didn't make any sense to me. I couldn't believe it. Nestor kept me in the parlor while Florian fetched Gloriana."

"There was no screaming?" I asked. "You don't remember hearing Florian yell when he found your wife?"

"No, no. It was a quiet thing. The death swept through like fog. We spoke in whispers. I can't explain it, but that was how it happened. I felt like the air was sucked from my lungs the moment I heard. Sucked from the room, as well. There was no air. No air for any of us. It sounds strange describing it, but the moment was suffocating, and I think we all felt it. Death came on a strained whisper."

I tried to make something of Astaire's retelling of his discovery. There was a ring of truth to it, and now that he'd told it, the intensity of grief had lessened, and a soft but heavy sadness blanketed me.

If Haven was still alive when Astaire left their room, and Florian was the one who found her body...

"What happened once Florian fetched Gloriana?" I asked.

"The innkeeper took over, and I am so grateful she did. A competent woman, it turns out. She didn't ask a million questions, just launched into action. She made the three of us wait in the parlor, went to confirm that Haven was dead, and then sent off the emergency owl asking for assistance."

"You were in the parlor from that point until when Nora and I arrived?"

"I suppose so. Honestly, I— I'm having a hard time remembering. I think I tried to go see my wife a few times, and Nestor was forced to subdue me. I wasn't thinking straight. Most likely, I'm still not thinking straight."

We'd reached the end of the timeline, and I couldn't think of anything else I ought to ask him. I was pretty sure I was mostly a babysitter while Nora did her own investigation around the body, and perhaps all she expected of me was to learn what emotions Astaire was experiencing. In that case, I had more than done my job here. The air around him carried a cloud of grief, regret, guilt, and plain ol' sadness. Exactly what I would expect a husband to feel not long after losing his wife of fifty years.

But also what a killer could feel.

Turns out, emotions are complicated.

I tried to think of follow-up questions, what Nora might ask him here, but I came up blank.

And then, another emotion caught my attention. It took me a moment to name the precise flavor of it, but slowly it emerged, buried beneath the other emotions: disgust. But not *just* disgust: loathing. Who did Astaire loathe, and why?

Before I could poke around for answers, a final question popped into my head, one I couldn't believe I'd almost forgotten to ask. "Astaire, did you order flowers from Time to Kiln for your wife this morning?"

He lifted his head from his hands. His eyes were puffy again, and the tears shone on his palms. "What?"

"The flowers outside your door. Did you order those for Haven?"

The corners of his mouth turned down. "No. I didn't order any flowers. I saw those outside the door when I was leaving, but I assumed there had been some sort of mistake and they were intended for another guest. Were they for Haven? Did someone *else* send my wife flowers?"

I held up a hand to stop that unpleasant train of thought from picking up steam. "No, we don't know that. You're probably right and whoever ordered them got the room wrong. There was no name on them that I know of. Not a sender or an intended recipient. You have enough on your mind. Don't worry about that."

He returned his head to his hands, gladly following my suggestion.

But I *did* worry about it. The order had been clear that the flowers were for Room D. Had they gotten it wrong, or had someone else sent flowers to Haven Featherbreeze on the day of her death?

Chapter Seven

Nora met me outside in the hallway as I was carefully shutting the door behind me to give Astaire time to grieve alone.

"Gloriana locked up Room D," Nora said. "She promised no one will go in or out until a deputy or Ted arrives. You find out anything interesting?"

I cast a look over my shoulder at the study door and nodded for her to follow me farther down the hall before briefing her.

"We definitely need to speak with Nestor and Florian," she said once I'd finished. "It sounds like Florian had the opportunity to murder Haven when he left the parlor, even if we're not sure why on earth he would want to. Or even how he would've done it. I didn't see any obvious injuries on Haven while I was in there with her, did you?"

I shook my head.

"Possibly a curse, then," Nora concluded. "Whenever Ted and Tanner arrive, they'll take the body back to the

Medical Examiner and the Magical Examiner. Hopefully, that can tell us what happened to her."

"If it was a spell," I replied, "then Florian has the means. He and Nestor are witches."

"I hate to stereotype," said Nora, "since there are kinds of magic that non-witches can do, but you're probably right." She leaned closer. "They're not the only witches here, though."

"Gloriana?" I said. "You think she might've done it?"

"And you." She winked. "I think we can rule you out by the timeline. But I don't know what I think yet about the rest. Gloriana is so far unaccounted for during the window of opportunity. Astaire was sitting with Florian and Nestor for a while before Florian found Haven. A powerful enough spell to kill someone doesn't take much time at all, just a flick of a wand. Assuming there was no one else in the house that we don't know about, it could've been Florian, Gloriana, or Wayne, depending on what kind of creature he turns out to be. We still need to meet him. But first, I think we'd better talk to Florian and Nestor."

"Can I ask you something?"

"Of course."

I felt silly asking it, but I was too curious. "Why are you and I the ones doing this investigation? Couldn't we just make sure everybody stays here until Tanner or Deputy Manchester can make it out?"

"It's a fair question," she said, "and coming from our old realm, I understand why you would ask that. But things run a little differently here. I'm not a deputy, but I might as well be at this point. I step in on murder cases when Tanner and Stu are busy, which is usually all the time. The High Council won't shell out for another deputy's pay, and they know I usually work for free on this sort of thing."

"And why do you work for free?"

Nora looked at me closely. "I don't need the money, and the dead need a voice. My hope is that we can find Haven's spirit somewhere in this place as we're asking around, and she might be able to help us."

I felt slightly ashamed now. Nora had such a clear sense of purpose and responsibility that motivated her, and there I was wanting to hand it right over to the first person in uniform I could find.

Not knowing what else to say, I nodded.

"Besides," she continued, holding up her hands and looking around, "don't you feel how different this place is? Tanner is a talented witch, but he's a West Wind. His magical talent is with things that grow from the earth. Whatever is going on in this place, it seems more in our wheelhouse."

She was right. I couldn't deny it. Perhaps we were the best suited for this job, even if we didn't have uniforms and a badge.

We found Florian and Nestor in the parlor downstairs, seated next to each other on a small loveseat by the fire. They had a soft knitted blanket wrapped around them both as they held each other comfortingly. A part of me ached to have someone who would be there for me like that in a similar situation. Maybe someday Dante—

No. A silly hope. The best indicator of the future is

the past, and I'd never had something like that before. Hoping it magically appeared for me was silliness.

Then again, if magic were to happen, it would be in Eastwind.

"Florian?" Nora said as we entered the sitting room.

The fair-skinned witch looked up at us, his blue eyes large and watery. "Yes?"

"And you're Nestor?" Nora asked the witch next to him.

"I am." The man's tight expression spoke volumes. His sandy skin was taut around his lips, and his onyx eyes made it clear that if we chose to harass the man he loved, we wouldn't like what followed. His animosity hit me like a shockwave, and I struggled to keep my feet under me as we approached them and I settled into one of the two open chairs by the fire.

I was more than happy to take a backseat in this interview and let Nora take the lead. "I understand you've had quite the shock today," she said, addressing Florian.

"I'll be fine," he said. But I noticed that he was shivering beneath the blanket where it draped over his shoulders.

"I'm afraid we have to ask you a few questions."

"I understand," said Florian.

Nestor did not look like a man who understood, as he aimed his glare squarely at Nora. "You're not the deputy. You're just his wife. Why are you asking us questions? And why should we answer anything you ask us?"

"If we're being precise, you're asking me questions at the moment," she said. "And I'm taking over because I have the authority to. The High Council grants me that under Article 138, Section H, Paragraphs—"

"Please, spare me. Fine, you have some sort of emergency jurisdiction. I get it. Go ahead."

Nora flashed a forced grin. "Do you remember what time this morning Astaire came down to join you two in this parlor?"

"Maybe ten thirty, ten forty-five. Something like that," said Florian softly.

"There's no clock in the parlor," Nestor added. "The whole point of going on vacation is to lose track of time. We weren't paying close attention."

"When he came down," Nora continued. "How did he seem to you?"

"You're asking about his affect?" replied Florian. He deferred to his husband with a look.

I was starting to get a clear picture of the dynamic, but I didn't know what it might indicate, if anything.

"He didn't strike me as a man who had just murdered his wife, if that's what you're asking," said Nestor.

"That's not necessarily what I'm asking," Nora replied, and I was glad she was taking the lead here. I didn't think I could go toe-to-toe with Nestor's hostile vibe like she could. I had a feeling she'd confronted much more hostile things in her time in Eastwind, though, many of which weren't living. "I'm asking you to describe what he was like when he came down here."

"He was angry," said Florian. "Angry and flustered. Possibly even bewildered."

"Women can do that to men," Nestor added scornfully. "They have a bewildering effect."

Nora smiled. "I take that as a compliment. What did he say, initially, when he joined the two of you in the parlor?"

"He was polite enough. He asked if he could join us, instead of just barging in," Nestor replied. "We said of course he could. It's a common space. We don't own it."

"I wouldn't have agreed to it if I'd known what would come next," added Florian. "He started talking and wouldn't stop. We were simply trying to enjoy our tea in peace."

I remembered passing the parlor on my way out with Dante much earlier that day and seeing Florian and Nestor sitting there in silence. "Enjoy" wasn't a word I would've used. If anything, they should've been grateful for the interruption of their silent tension.

"What specifically did he talk about?" Nora asked.

Florian pulled the blanket tighter around him, and in doing so, it slipped partially off Nestor. Nestor gave it a hard tug to get his portion of it back, then replied, "He said his wife was needy and wanted more attention than any sane person could ask for from another."

"Have you ever reached the point," Florian said, "where you're so annoyed with someone that every little thing they do is a strike against their character?"

Nora didn't answer, but instead replied, "That was the state Astaire was in when he came down?"

"Absolutely," said Florian. "And we had to hear all about it. Haven was selfish. She showered in the morning before him without even asking. Her makeup took too much counter space. Her voice was like a banshee's. I wouldn't have been shocked to hear him complain that she took too many breaths per minute. The man was fed up with her very existence."

"But not in a way that made it seem like he'd already

done something about it," Nestor added. "He was a man desperate to figure out *what* to do about it."

Nora nodded along. "And when did you get up and leave the room, Florian?"

He avoided making eye contact with either one of us as he said, "Hmm... ah, well, I don't know the exact time, but I do remember it being when he started talking about Haven's mother."

"And why did you get up?" she asked.

Astaire had presumed it was to use the restroom, but I suspected there was another driving force behind it.

"I couldn't take it anymore," Florian said, confirming my suspicion. "Nestor has the ability to speak truth easily, but I just... I start having these bitter thoughts about people, and they build up so quickly that if I were to say even one, I fear I would reveal them all and it would be too much. Astaire was clearly in a state after arguing with Haven, and I didn't want to unload on him. So, I got up and walked out."

"Sounds like a wise idea," said Nora. "And where did you go?"

He shrugged. "Out. Out of earshot of his complaining."

"But where?" she persisted.

"I wandered around a bit. I don't know. I ended up back in our room for a moment, stared out the window to let my thoughts settle, and then wondered if it was safe to return to the parlor."

"Florian," Nora said gently, "it's quite important that you're completely honest about where you went after leaving the room."

Florian didn't speak right away. Instead, his eyes

darted briefly to his husband. "The kitchen," he said finally.

"The kitchen?" Nora repeated. "Why?"

I had the same question. Why not just say he was going to the kitchen? There was nothing suspicious about wanting a snack.

Nestor answered for him. "He was getting a snack. Weren't you, Flor?"

Looking chastened, Florian nodded. "I'm an emotional eater. Whenever I get annoyed, I find myself eating. Nestor can't stand it."

I tried to understand what was so wrong about emotional eating. Were there people who *didn't* want a cookie every time they were sad, ashamed, annoyed, or angry? How strange!

I was learning all kinds of things in this town.

"It's not a healthy way of coping," Nestor replied. "If you have energy to burn, go for a run."

"A run?" Florian blurted. "Have you *ever* in our years together seen me *go for a run?* You're clearly confused about who you married."

"Not at all. I married a fit witch. What I'm confused about is who *you* are and what you did with him."

Nora and I shared a wide-eyed look. Neither one of us wanted to get involved in this.

"I ate him," Florian replied, rubbing his belly. "Couldn't you tell by looking at me? I was so annoyed living with you that I kept eating and eating until I'd swallowed down every last bit of him!"

Not that my opinion mattered, but I didn't find Florian to be abnormally large at all. In fact, he appeared slightly slimmer around the middle than Nestor.

I suspected Nora was having the same thoughts, and she watched their continuing back and forth like a tennis spectator sitting quietly in the stands.

Oh no, she wasn't expecting *me* to intervene, was she?

Thankfully, neither of us had to be the one to step in, because a polite knock on the front door echoed through the downstairs and cut the bickering short.

Chapter Eight

Gloriana answered the door, and a moment later, I heard a familiar, scratchy voice. "Hope I'm not interrupting."

"Ted," Nora said, standing, and I was happy to leave the parlor to follow her into the entryway and greet the reaper.

A large portion of the heaviness of Muscoff Manor Inn lifted from over me the moment I laid eyes on Ted. He was like a ray of sunshine in this place. I had lost sight of the oppressiveness I was swimming in until he arrived and cut through it like a knife. Or a scythe.

Speaking of scythes, he thumped the base of his on the ground a few times to knock off some of the snow from outside. "Hello Nora and Dahlia!" He waved, even though we were only a few feet away from him. "Sorry I took so long getting here. I only had a couple of clues left on my crossword, and then I had my tab open at Medium Rare and I didn't want to leave without saying goodbye to Bryant."

"Your timing is actually perfect," Nora said, casting a

quick look back toward the room where Nestor and Florian were still seated. "And for what it's worth, I think Bryant knows you like him. And if you ever had to split on a tab, that's okay too. I know you're good for it the next time you come in."

"Oh wow, thanks! That makes me feel better. And I'm definitely good for the money! I don't even remember how I filled the time each day before Medium Rare opened. It's my favorite place outside of my own home." He leaned toward me and added, "I have a flock of phoenixes that's roosting in my cabin for the winter. It's a fun time. Mudbug—that's my cat—she loves them. And they can't accidentally set her on fire because she's a ghost." He chuckled. "Life really works out the way it's supposed to, doesn't it?"

It seemed like a strange thing to say at a murder scene, but I understood his sentiment and nodded along.

"Shall I show you to the body?" Gloriana asked.

Ted turned to Nora. "Has Tanner or Stu been by yet?"

"Nope. Best if you leave the body where it's at until they get a look around. Tanner should be over soon."

"Amazing. I love that guy. Any sign of the spirit?"

"None yet," Nora replied. "I'll let you know if I see something. Maybe best not to cart her away until I can have a word with her."

"Got it." He gave her a salute with a gloved hand, and then Gloriana led him upstairs.

Once they were out of sight, Nora said, "Did you get anything interesting off Nestor and Flor—"

Another knock on the door, this one much louder.

Nora answered it. Tanner's professional expression

lit up as soon as he saw who was on the other side of the threshold. "Good goddess, you are stunning."

"We're working, Tanner." She did a poor job of hiding her grin.

"Who said I'm not here to serve and protect?" He stomped his boots on the rug, then stole a quick kiss from her.

I tried not to watch, but it was hard not to. Tanner was a serious authority in town, and he was good at what he did, but he turned into a doting schoolboy every time he saw his wife. The way the two of them got along was something I enjoyed watching, not in a weird way, but in an aspirational one. I did my best not to envy them for what they had.

"She leaving all the grunt work to you again?" Tanner asked me.

"No, she's doing most of it. I'm just learning from the master."

He laughed, and Nora rolled her eyes.

Tanner appeared to be about to speak again, but then he paused, and his brows pinched together as a shudder ran through him. "What *is* that?"

It was obvious what he meant. The feeling started to settle in as soon as you stepped inside the place. If it had a color, it'd be a smoggy gray. I'd gotten used to it so quickly that I'd almost forgotten about it until Ted arrived and was like a fresh ocean breeze cutting through it, but now it was back.

"It's bad," Nora replied. "I don't know what it is, exactly, but I feel it, too."

"Sadness?" he said. "No, that's not quite it." He shuddered again.

"Maybe you ought to get some staurolite for your-self," Nora said. "It keeps you grounded against stray energy like this."

Whatever it was, it was clearly taking a heavy toll on him. His regular cheery demeanor had been replaced by a look of extreme discomfort. I hated to see him like that, since his lightness was one of my favorite things about him. So, I did the only thing I could do. After all, he'd been so generous to me since the moment I landed in Eastwind. I could handle a little negative energy if it meant giving him a break.

Or so I thought.

"You can borrow mine," I said, wrapping my fingers around the chain of the staurolite pendant. "It'll help you stay focused on the investigation."

"I don't think that's a good idea," Nora said.

The moment I pulled the chain over my head, I proved her suspicions right.

I'd had no idea just how much the staurolite had been protecting me. The smoggy feeling turned from gray to black, and an avalanche of emotions threatened to bury me. It felt like the manor was crumbling around me, falling onto my head and shoulders, crushing me beneath it. Guilt, rage, sorrow, glee, and deep, deep loneliness fell around me until I couldn't see a thing in the swirl of it.

They wanted in. The emotions. They were trying to find a way inside me, and I knew they would soon. I struggled against it, though. That was not my grief. That was not my rage. That was not my sorrow.

Or was it? It became more and more difficult to tell. Maybe it was. Maybe all of those things had been inside me the whole time and now they were waking up...

"Dahlia! Dahlia! Can you hear me?"

The smog thinned until I could see Nora's face only a foot away from mine. I blinked.

We were no longer in the entryway. I was staring at the ceiling.

"Where am I?" I asked.

"Oh, thank goddess." She sighed. "You're just in the parlor. You collapsed in the entryway, and Tanner brought you in here."

"Tanner?" I looked around and found him seated on a chair across the room. His arms were folded over his chest, and he stared at me with a look of concern I didn't like at all.

I groaned and covered my eyes with my hand. "I didn't make a scene, did I?"

"You did," she said, "but we were the only ones who saw it. What happened?"

"It's hard to explain."

Tanner approached Nora, "You got this?"

"I think so. You go meet Ted upstairs. I'll holler if I need anything."

Before he left, he placed a hand on my shoulder and said, "I appreciate what you were trying to do, but please keep that thing on you at all times while you're here." He motioned toward my chest where the staurolite pendant rested once again. "I've been in dark moods before; I can manage it again while I'm here."

I nodded. I had no desire to take the pendant off if it meant I'd be back where I'd been a moment earlier. I never wanted to be in that place again.

"I'm sorry," I said. "I had no idea that would happen."

"None of us did," Nora replied.

"You said it wasn't a good idea, and I didn't listen."

Nora let out a puff of air. "Don't give me so much credit. I had no idea what would happen. I thought maybe you'd feel a little extra morose. I had no idea it would cause you to collapse."

"I don't remember collapsing," I said. "I just remember the feelings closing in, and then I woke up here."

"What feelings?" she asked.

"All kinds of feelings. Dark ones. Even the glee felt bitter and dark."

"Hmm..." She was silent for a moment. "I knew you were sensitive to emotions when you got here, but I think I've underestimated it. That's my fault since certain emotions could slap me in the face and I wouldn't notice. But it looks like your powers are quite something. Maybe even beyond my ability to help you with." She frowned. "Tanner's right. Keep that staurolite on at all times. There are a lot of energies swirling around Eastwind, and you want to keep them *outside* of you, if at all possible."

"I couldn't agree more," I said, a throb settling in at my temples.

"How did you know to wear staurolite before you knew you were a Fifth Wind?" she asked. "I still don't understand that."

"A friend gave it to me at a shop, back in my other realm."

"On Earth, right?" There was a tone of hesitation to her voice that I didn't understand. I tried to tune into her emotions, but I was getting nothing off her. It was like she'd shut it all off.

"Right. Where you're from."

"Texas?"

"Oh. No. I'm not from Texas. I'm from New Orleans."

Nora's face drained of color instantly.

"What? What is it?" I forced myself to sit up despite the throbbing in my head. "Is there something wrong with New Orleans?"

It looked like she was bracing herself against something unpleasant as she asked, "Did you happen to get that pendant at a place called The South Wind?"

Now it was my turn to be surprised. "Yes! You've been there?"

She pressed a finger to her lips to quiet me down. "I've been there." A quick check over her shoulder to make sure we were alone, then, "Is Donovan still there?"

My eyes shot open. The name made my heart ache. Donovan. Would I ever see him again? He was one of my only friends prior to coming here, and I hadn't appreciated him while I could. "He is," I said, making sure to keep my voice low, though not understanding why this was something to be whispered. "He's one of the people who gave me the necklace."

"And how... how is he?" she asked.

I was surprised by the wave of sadness from her that accompanied the question. "Good, I guess."

"He seems happy?"

"Oh, sure. That was the impression I always got, at least. He and his wife seem in love and all that."

A smile blossomed on Nora's face. "His wife? That wouldn't be Angelina, would it?"

"Yes! Did you know her, too?"

"I did."

"From before you came here?" I asked.

"No, they're from Eastwind."

"Eastwind?!" I blurted, and again she pressed a finger to her lips.

"It's a long story."

"How did they get there?" I asked. "You're telling me I could go back to New Orleans? I'm not trapped here?"

"Technically, yes, there's a way." She watched me closely as she asked, "Do you want to go back?"

I opened my mouth then snapped it shut as my brain caught up. "Not really," I said.

"Then it's a non-issue."

"Angelina and Donovan are from here? Is that how they knew to give me the staurolite? They'd seen you wearing it?"

"That would be my guess. I don't know how they could tell you needed it, but I'm glad they did. Angelina's real name is Evangeline, by the way. She went by Eva here, but she was born in New Orleans, like you. She died and found herself in Eastwind. So, when she went back, she couldn't very well say she was the same person who was buried and gone. That's one of the complications of going back."

"Was Donovan born there, too?"

Nora swallowed hard. "No. He was born here. The Stringfellows, his parents, still live here. It's probably best not to talk about him out and about for that reason. Tanner told them what happened, but they don't quite understand. It's... It's messy."

"Tanner knows him too," I murmured. I was really struggling to get my head around this clash of worlds.

"He does. They were best friends for most of their

life. Tanner's parents died when he was younger, and the Stringfellows were there for him."

"Then Tanner probably wants to hear that Donovan is doing okay, too."

Nora patted me on the shoulder where I sat on the sofa. "I think you should leave that to me. I'll tell him... when the time is right. It's, well, it's a complicated dynamic. He was good friends with Eva when they lived together in New Orleans, too, so—"

"Hold on, Tanner lived in New Orleans?"

Nora sighed. "Like I said. Complicated. But I'm glad to hear Donovan and Eva are still doing well. And that they're together. I always thought she was good for him."

Movement behind Nora caught my attention. Gloriana was shuffling in with a tea tray, Givens slinking so close at her heels I wondered how he didn't get kicked.

"I've just heard about the collapse." She set the tray on the table next to me. "Are you okay?"

"I'm fine," I said, embarrassed by the attention. "Much better, thank you."

"Whatever happened?" She poured me a cup of the tea and muttered, "peppermint and chamomile" as she shoved it into my hand. I wasn't sure how much more tea I could handle in a day, but it smelled wonderful.

"Just a little faint," Nora answered for me. "She forgot to eat lunch."

"Oh!" Gloriana's brows shot up. "Should I have Wayne fix something for her?"

"That would be generous of Wayne. Before you speak with him, would you mind sitting for a moment? We're curious about a few things."

After the last couple of hours, I was curious about

more than a few things, but I was excited to see what Nora was up to.

Gloriana sat on a stuffed ottoman and folded her hands in her lap. Her familiar curled up on her toes, keeping a close eye on me. "What can I help you with?"

"I'm curious about the exterior doors to the inn. How many are there?"

"Three," she replied. "The front door, a side door leading off the kitchen for deliveries, and one emergency door on the top floor that leads to a fire escape."

"And guests could theoretically go in or out of any of these when they wanted?"

"They can leave whenever they want, but the doors lock automatically from the inside. Unless you have a key, you can't get back in without someone letting you in."

"You're the only one with a key?"

"No. Wayne has one, too. He runs a lot of errands to keep the kitchen operational."

"Hmm..." said Nora. "That limits our potential suspects to those already at the inn at the time of the murder and anyone else they might've let in. So, it could be anyone."

"Ah," said Gloriana. "I can help you with that. No one comes in and out without me knowing. The doors are spelled so that I feel a slight tickle in my arm every time they open and close. It would be irresponsible of an innkeeper not to keep track of who is in the inn." She smiled.

"Were there any unaccounted-for tickles today?" Nora asked.

"The only one on the front door was not long ago, when you let Tanner inside. I was upstairs with Ted, and

I even said, 'Oh, I think Tanner has just arrived.' I feel the front door here." She tapped a spot on her left bicep. "I haven't felt anything from the emergency exit in weeks—no one uses that door—and I've felt the kitchen door open and shut at all the usual times." She tapped a spot on her forearm.

"And what are the usual times?" Nora asked.

"Twice in the morning, when Wayne fetches fresh produce and meats from the Emporium for the day's meals. Sometimes Wayne forgets an ingredient and must return to the Emporium to get it." She leaned forward and whispered, "He's a fabulous cook, but a little scatter-brained at times."

"No other doors opening throughout the day that you know about?"

"None."

"And what about the windows?" asked Nora.

Gloriana smiled. "Warded. No one can go out or in through the windows. It's a legal requirement for any hotel, inn, or facility that rents rooms to the public. Guests feel safer when they know nothing is creeping into their room through the window at night."

"I didn't know that," Nora said.

"Why would you? You live here. You don't need to stay at an inn or hotel." Gloriana smiled pleasantly, but I felt nothing close to friendliness coming from her.

As I sipped my tea (it was delicious and exactly the boost I needed to lift my spirits in this place), Nora said, "I need you to tell me everyone who's staying here right now. I know you don't want to give away guest privacy, but it's important. If there were no other doors opening, as you say, then we can narrow down our suspects once I have the list. The sooner we do that, the sooner we can get out of your hair and let you continue conducting your business."

"I'm afraid—"

Feeling newly invigorated, I cut her off. "We already know about Haven, Astaire, Florian, Nestor, Wayne, you, and Sheriff Bloom," I said, counting off the names on my fingers. "Are there others?"

Gloriana shot me a resentful look, but said, "No, that's the complete list of guests at the moment. It's not many, but we're still a fairly new establishment. I'm sure the place will begin booking up regularly before long."

"Gabby Bloom is staying alone?" Nora asked, and I understood why she would. This was supposed to be a couples' retreat.

"She is," replied Gloriana. "And she prefers to be left completely alone. It was her one request."

"You mentioned that," said Nora. "We'll need to speak with Wayne."

"You're entirely welcome to. Speaking of him,"—she stood, narrowly avoiding stepping on her familiar's tail as she did—"I'd better check to make sure he's put all the dishes away after lunch. If you'll excuse me."

Once she was gone, Nora said, "Normally, I'd say you and I could split up to speak with everyone, but I think we're better together. I know the questions to ask, and you can tell what emotions are hiding behind the facades. By the way, you get anything off Gloriana?"

I shook my head. "She doesn't give off much. I can feel it when someone enters a room because there's a slight change. Like the chemistry has shifted. But when she enters the room, it's not like that. It's like she blends right in. Like adding more water to a bucket of water. It doesn't change the chemistry."

I felt relief in finally putting this understanding into words. I'd been sensing it more and more as my powers seemed to intensify (or I became more sensitive to them), but it was tricky to explain.

It had been nagging at my subconscious that nothing changed when Gloriana and her familiar entered a room, but until Nora had asked, I hadn't brought the niggle to my conscious mind.

"What do you think that means?" I asked.

Nora chuckled. "You'll have to tell me. I don't understand your powers *at all*."

She offered me a hand to help me to my feet.

"There's certainly something strange about this place," she said. "I don't know what yet, but it's undeniable. Perhaps if we figure it out, we'll have a better understanding of what happened to Haven."

"Perhaps we should sit down with Gloriana once more to get a full timeline of her morning," I suggested. "She pops up and then leaves, and we haven't really interviewed her."

Nora grinned. "You couldn't be more right. It could *always* be the butler."

Chapter Nine

"No sign of a murder weapon," Tanner said once we joined him upstairs in Room D. "No hex bags, broken objects, ritual daggers, mimic dolls, or anything. I also don't see any visible signs of injury, and my preliminary sweep didn't find traces of spell work."

Someone had placed a blanket over Haven, and we stood next to it as Tanner caught us up.

"What does that leave?" I asked.

He tucked his wand into his duty belt and sighed. "Not sure. Poison? A medical event? Possibly a spell that's too subtle for my wand to detect. The magical examiner has better tools for that sort of thing."

A door closed in the hall, pulling my attention from Tanner. Sheriff Bloom paused in the hall, just outside the doorway, still in her robe and slippers. She looked like she was about to say something helpful, but when her gaze fell on Tanner, she said, "Nope. Not getting involved. I'm not here. I don't see anything." Then she kept walking.

I turned to Tanner, who appeared horrified. "Sheriff Bloom is here?" he said.

Nora nodded.

"And she's... walking around in a robe?"

"Seems like it."

He paused, staring out into the hallway. "Is she here *with* someone?"

"Nope," Nora replied.

Tanner's shoulders relaxed, and his look of horror faded. "Okay. I know it's none of my business, but I'm glad to hear it."

"Why, would you be jealous?" Nora teased.

"Oh. come on, you know what I mean. Who would be good enough for Sheriff Bloom?"

Nora shrugged. "Can't argue with you there."

Ted peeked his head into the room. "Still no signs of her spirit?"

As Nora waved him in, she said, "None yet. You haven't found her?"

"Nope. Maybe she's waiting back at my cabin. That happens sometimes. If they don't have unfinished business, they float there to meet me. I have no clue how they know to do that, though. Heh." He waved his scythe gently, and a long oaken box appeared outside the doorway. It floated inside the room before making a gentle landing right next to the body. "My new toy," Ted said proudly. "What do you think?"

Tanner nodded approvingly. "Definitely more discreet than dragging a body in a bag," he said.

"That's what I said! Who's to say what's in the box, right? Could be anything."

I decided not to mention that the context clue of the town's reaper might give it away.

"Ezra custom ordered this for me," Ted continued, beaming proudly at the box. "It works with my specific brand of magic. Not cheap. Not cheap at all. But I've had centuries to build my savings, so I thought, heck, why not splurge on something? And if it's something that gives the people in the town I love a little more dignity when they die, even better!"

"I think it's a great investment and a lovely sentiment," Nora said.

Once Ted had Haven loaded up, he said, "Do you think her husband would like to say goodbye?"

"That's a kind thought," Tanner said, "but we'd better get her to the medical and magical examiners before we let anyone else have access to her."

"Oh right. The murder. Heh. Good call."

As Ted left the room with the body, I couldn't help but marvel at how irrelevant he seemed to find the cause of death. Perhaps to a reaper, death was death, and the way it happened mattered less. There was something peaceful in that idea, but I couldn't put my finger on it.

Astaire was in the same room where I'd left him, sitting in the chair by the fire, when Nora and I tracked him down for further questioning.

He hardly seemed to notice us as we sat near him. His glassy gaze remained on the crackling fire.

I wasn't sure what else Nora wanted to know that I hadn't already covered, so I listened closely.

"Ted's just left with Haven," Nora said. "Once the

checks are complete, you'll be able to have a proper funeral for her."

He said nothing.

"Astaire, I know you and Haven are from Avalon, but is there anyone staying here who she might've known previous to arriving?"

The question was provocative enough to pull his attention from the fire, and he stared at Nora, blinking. "I certainly don't know anyone here. Perhaps she knew someone, but I can't imagine who. She's never been to Eastwind before. Not to my knowledge, at least."

"Did she have any particular interactions with the other guests during your time here that might've caused tension?"

"No. She was ornery since we arrived, but only to me. She was her usual jovial self to everyone else. She wants —wanted attention above all else, and she would be whoever she needed to be to get it. She preferred positive attention, but she'd take negative attention if that was all she could get."

"And was that all she could get with the other guests?"

"No, no." He waved away the idea. "She could get plenty of positive attention from them. She always wanted more attention than I could give, than any single person could give."

"And did it make you jealous?" Nora asked.

"No, and that's the truth of it. I know you're trying to find a reason why I might've killed her, and in some ways, I wish I could give it to you so we could be done with this. But I didn't murder my wife, and I wasn't jealous when other men and women noticed her and gave her attention. She was a beautiful woman, no debating that. When I saw others eyeing her in that way, all I felt was relief. As long as they were giving her attention, she wouldn't be demanding it from me, and I could focus on other things without her badgering me." He moaned. "Oh, that's so terrible of me to say. So, so terrible. I loved her, I really did. How could I speak like that of her?" He pressed his fingertips to his forehead. "I've got to get out of here. I can't stand being in this inn for another second!"

Nora nodded. "I need you to stay in Eastwind for now, but I can arrange a place for you to stay. There's a lodge not far from here owned by the head of the were-bear clan."

"Werebears? You expect me to stay with werebears? Did I come to Eastwind or Wisconsin?"

It was so strange to hear a familiar location mentioned, that I snapped my attention to Nora, who shook her head minutely and whispered, "Not that one. There's a realm. I'll explain later."

She returned her attention to Astaire. "No one will bother you while you're there. You can have all the peace and quiet you want outside of any conversations the deputies might need to have with you."

Astaire sounded like the embodiment of misery itself when he said, "Very well."

Nora told him to hang tight, and then we both left the study.

Beside the front door was a small wooden table on spindly legs. A small stack of parchment pieces lay in a metal holder, and she took one out, jotted a message on it with the pen resting on the table, and then folded it up. "Darius Pine," she said, opening the front door so that we were met with a bitter reminder of the season. Just below the porch light was a brass perch, and on it sat a sleeping owl, its feathers gathering flakes of downy snow. Nora poked the bird gently to rouse it then held out the folded parchment. The owl snatched it in its talons and then took off into the trees. "Darius is the head of the Eastwind werebears and a friend of mine. He's generous to the bone. I'm sure he'll put Astaire up for as long as we need in one of his cabins."

That was all good to know, but my mind was too caught up on an unrelated detail to focus entirely. "Was the owl there the whole time?" I pointed to the perch.

Nora shrugged. "I hope not. It's cold." She nodded for us to step back inside, then she shut out the frigid air.

"It just happened to be there when you needed it. Lucky."

"I don't think it's a matter of luck," she said. "No one really knows how the owl post works, only that it does. The owls know where they'll be needed and when. If one isn't around when you need it, that's either because they're all busy, which happens sometimes when something big goes down, or the thing you're about to send is such a bad idea that they are trying to give you time to reconsider sending it."

As I listened, unsure how much of that was true and how much was Eastwind legend, I had the strangest desire to be an owl.

Nora tapped at her lips, thinking. "I think we ought to have a look around the place and see if we can locate Haven. It's rare that spirits remember who killed them, since it tends to be a bit of a shock, but every now and again they remember. If we can wrap this thing up before dinner, I'll take you up to Stews & Brews for a nice steak."

I nodded along with the plan, but then added, "I've had a lot of tea today. I think I need to make a pit stop."

Nora chuckled. "Right. You gotta build up a tolerance to so much tea on investigations. It seems like it comes from every direction. I'm gonna poke around by Room D, see if I can find her. There's a restroom just down that hallway. I'll meet you upstairs."

I found the restroom without any trouble and was relieved to find it was a welcoming space with cheery powder pink wallpaper and bright lights above the mirror.

Yes, I did need to let some of the tea out of my system, but it wasn't by any means an emergency. Mostly, I'd been desperate to be alone. My insides felt like they were crawling with emotions after the interview with Astaire, and while I felt the urge to cry, nothing came when I gave myself the space to. I simply felt unsettled, and the only thing my brain was telling me to do about it was to go find somewhere to be alone. And so there I was, staring at myself in the mirror as I washed my hands as slowly as possible.

It was entirely possible, I realized as I dried my hands on the hand towel and stepped back into the hallway, that I wasn't cut out for this sort of work. Nora seemed to think I was, but if I was going to be tossed around by the strong emotions of each person we spoke with, I might not be able to withstand it for long. I certainly wouldn't be at the top of my game. Perhaps I was too sensitive to be any good at this and ought to tell her I was out, that I appreciated all her wisdom and insight into being a Fifth

Wind, but I could no longer absorb it on the job. Maybe over breakfast at her house. Or we could meet up for coffee at A New Leaf every week. Yes, that would be much better. More suited to my sensitivities. A latte and chocolate croissant.

I felt my muscles begin to relax at the thought of routine, of coziness, of *not murder*. That was a life I would be grateful for every day. Wake up, work at the studio, learn a little from Nora over a hot coffee, improve my pottery skills, and maybe even have time and money to wind down at night at Sheehan's Pub. If Nora genuinely needed an assistant in what she did, almost anyone in this town would make a better one than me.

"Oops, sorry!" Lost in my own head, I'd turned a corner and walked straight into—

No, not into. *Through.*

The chill registered belatedly as I turned on my heels to stare at what, or rather who, I had just walked through.

This was only the second ghost I'd ever encountered. I was far from desensitized to the strangeness of it. "I'm so sorry. I didn't see you there."

Like the first spirit I'd encountered, this one appeared to be a woman. But unlike the first one, this one was an elf.

It didn't take a genius to put the pieces together. "Haven?"

She was wide-eyed, her head whipping this way and that like a deer on high alert. "Where did he go?"

"Who?" I asked, checking quickly over my shoulder. Nothing was there. Phew! The hair on my arms didn't get the memo, though, and it continued to stand on end.

Haven's eyes crossed slightly as she focused them on me. "You can see me?"

"Yes. Haven, you were murdered. Somebody killed you. I need to know who—"

"Don't let him find me," she said. "I beg you."

"Who?"

Her eyes grew wider. "He's near. You seem like a nice girl, so if you see him, stay away."

And before I could ask any further questions, the spirit darted off, disappearing into the air down the hallway.

I realized my mouth was hanging open and snapped it shut. Who was she talking about? Who was "he"? Unfortunately, there were a lot of hes hanging around, but one of them had Haven so scared she couldn't carry on a coherent conversation, even one as important as who murdered her.

What would scare someone so bad once they were already dead? Ted? Was she trying to avoid him finding her and taking her onto the next place?

I thought about following after her and searching around where she vanished in the hallway, trying to pin her down about whom she was avoiding, but I didn't know where to begin. She had disappeared. Would she appear somewhere nearby? In the same place she disappeared from? Or somewhere else entirely? (I really needed to check out some books at the library about ghost rules.)

But also, I wasn't that brave. I won't lie; her warnings freaked me out, and I felt a sudden urge to find someone familiar to stick myself to like glue. Perhaps I now knew how Atlas felt most of the time.

"What are you doing?"

I turned to find Nora walking up behind me. She appeared concerned.

"Huh?"

"I expected you to meet me upstairs, but after a long time passed, I thought I'd come check on you. You seem fine, so what are you up to? Did you get lost on your way to the kitchen?"

"I got a little sidetracked, but it hasn't been that long," I said.

She frowned. "It's been nearly half an hour since you went to use the restroom."

"No way," I said.

"According to the clock on the wall, yes way. I was worried you might've fallen in."

If I hadn't been so worried about the time I'd apparently lost, I might've giggled. "I found Haven."

I caught Nora up on the brief and baffling interaction, and she didn't seem any more excited about the prospect of a spirit running from someone than I did. But once I'd finished, she jumped to the same best-case conclusion I had. "She probably means Ted. Spirits avoid him sometimes."

"Do they usually look terrified?" I asked.

"Not generally, but I've seen it once or twice. The fear of the unknown can be the most powerful fear of all, and what comes next for a spirit after leaving the body is mostly unknown." She rolled her shoulders back. "Maybe we'll run into her again and can pin her down on an answer. In the meantime, we still need to speak with Wayne."

"He'll be in the kitchen, probably, right?" I said.

"It sounds like he lives there."

Feeling much more settled by the company, I inhaled deeply, and tried to reset my mind to the task at hand: yet another interview. Hopefully, no more tea pushed on me for at least a little while, though.

The door to the kitchen was through the dining room, and just as we approached it, it flung open and Gloriana stepped out, wiping wet hands on her cotton skirt. Givens scurried through before the door swung shut. "Looking for something?" she asked.

"Tea," Nora said, shooting me a conspiratorial sideways glance. "We can't get enough of it." I had to bite my lip to keep from smiling.

"I'll make some for you in just a moment. I'm afraid the owner is on his way over. Surprise visit. Terrible timing. Absolutely terrible. I'd hoped to have the murder straightened out before he ever learned of it."

"Is it possible that he's coming by *because* there's a murder?" Nora asked.

"Oh, what a terrible idea! I hate the thought. He's going to be so disappointed that I let this happen."

Nora and I shared a look as Gloriana breezed around us. Wayne could wait. We followed the innkeeper.

She passed straight through the entryway and proceeded into the parlor. "What a mess this place is! He won't approve. What a terrible impression he'll have. This is an exception, not the standard." She grabbed a pillow from one of the couches and beat it into fluffy submission. Across the room, Sheriff Bloom sat by the fire in her comfortable robe and slippers, reading a book. I caught a glimpse of the cover. It had *His Sinful Wings* written across it, partially covering a lean, shirtless angel who clutched a fawning woman to his chest.

Bloom glanced up from her book and caught me looking. She grinned. "One of Ruby's recommendations. I won't deny she has great taste in literature." She returned to her reading.

Meanwhile, Gloriana had worked herself into quite a state and was dragging her hand over every flat surface she could, kicking up only a few particles of dust into the air each time. The place was far from messy by any reasonable standards.

As the front door opened and Gloriana turned rapidly on her heels toward the sound, freezing in place. "He's here."

I peered through the open parlor door that looked out into the entryway, waiting to see *who* was here. In my mind, I imagined a monster with dripping fangs, razor claws, and a spiked tail designed for thrashing stomping into the parlor.

Yes, my imagination had a way of running away with me, but to be fair, the man who stepped into view was only slightly less intimidating.

"You?" said Nora.

"For fang's sake," cursed Bloom from her chair. "Can't I have a single peaceful vacation without it being absolutely ruined?"

The man in the doorway grinned proudly at the reception then locked his gaze onto me. "Dahlia Wildes," said Count Malavic. "What a pleasure to see you again."

Chapter Ten

"Nuh-uh." Gabby Bloom stood swiftly from her chair by the fire, setting *His Sinful Wings* aside as she strode across the room to confront the vampire. "Don't you dare try your nonsense on Dahlia just because she's new around here and you have a thing for death."

Malavic shrugged. "A man always wants what he cannot have." He looked Bloom up and down, his eyes lingering where the two sides of her robe formed a V below her collarbone. "I like this look on you. Reminds me of old times, when I got to see the softer side of you."

"You'll see the *in*side of a jail cell if you try anything with Dahlia, I promise you. I may be on vacation, but that doesn't mean I won't cuff you and lead you out of here."

Malavic held out his wrists for her. "Don't tempt me, you devil." He grinned.

Bloom looked like she was about to lay into him, then she paused, took a deep breath, and put her back to him. "You're on vacation, Gabby," she muttered to herself, walking to the chair and grabbing her book. "You can deal with his nefarious doings any other week of your life."

"I'm so sorry to have kept you from your smut," he said, catching sight of the book in her hand.

She headed for the exit, pausing right in front of him. Malavic was a tall man, but Gabby Bloom wasn't a single hair shorter. "Not all romance is smut, but I wouldn't expect you to know that."

His brows rose in amusement. "I wouldn't expect you to know it either."

She grunted and walked past him out the door, clipping his shoulder as she went.

Malavic chuckled, watched her go, then returned his attention to the parlor, where Nora, Gloriana and I watched the interaction unfold, not wanting to get in the middle of it. The vampire's expression darkened. "Terrible business, this murder."

"You know already?" Gloriana said breathlessly.

"Of course I know." He shrugged off his black wool coat and tossed it onto the nearest couch.

"Is the town already talking about it?" she asked.

"Thankfully, no. But I do hope to get this mess cleaned up before the word spreads. "'There was a murder at Muscoff Manor Inn... but it was a fluke and has been solved' poses far less of a threat to my investment in this place than, 'There was a murder at Muscoff Manor Inn... and the killer could still be lurking the halls.'"

Gloriana wrung her hands together. "I was hoping to get it cleared up before even you knew about it."

"That's why they're here, I presume." He nodded toward Nora and me.

"Precisely."

"And the body?" he asked.

"Already taken care of. Deputy Culpepper came by earlier."

"Aww," he said, tilting his head to the side and staring at Nora. "A couple that investigates together—"

Nora held up a hand. "You don't need to even try finishing that sentence with something cute. I don't care. I'm here to do what needs to be done, and if I'd known you were the owner of this place, I might've worked more slowly and dropped a hot tip to Flufferbum over at the *Eastwind Watch*."

Malavic's forced humor disappeared. "That werebunny is the bane of my existence. Did you happen to read the piece he wrote about me last month?"

Nora grinned. "One of my favorites. Did you really propose monetizing your dragon's lair as a kiddie attraction to raise money for the town's coffer?"

"Maggie is incredibly well trained. And I would obviously cover any medical or funeral expenses out of my own pocket. I'm a generous man, if nothing else."

"And yet the money that you hoard in your dragon's lair can't go to fund the town's basic budgetary items?"

He dismissed her with a flick of the wrist. "It's clear why you're not the treasurer of the High Council. You don't grasp basic concepts of public versus private." He seemed to float across the room as he walked, stopping just short of me and staring down into my face. I swallowed hard.

If one didn't know a thing about the kind of person he was, one might say Sebastian Malavic was dreamy. He had an intensity in his eyes that couldn't be denied. And when he was this close...

The passion consumed me like a waft of sweet perfume, and I felt irrevocably lost in it. All I could see was his face now. Why was he looking at me like that? What did he want? Whatever it was, he could have it.

The chain of my staurolite tugged gently at the back of my neck, snapping me out of it. Before I could even blink, Nora slapped the pendant out of Malavic's hand.

"None of that," she said. "You heard Bloom. Leave Dahlia alone."

Gloriana stepped forward. "I'm so sorry, Count. The way these women are treating you—"

"I would expect nothing less," he said, taking another step back from me, still grinning like he'd just won a competition I didn't realize I was participating in.

Nora shooed Malavic out of the parlor, grabbing his discarded coat and shoving it at him. "We'll solve this faster if you're out of the way, I can tell you that."

"Very well," he said, his back straight. "I appreciate both your expediency and your discretion." He turned to face her, slipping into his coat in a single slick motion. "If Flufferbum publishes a word about this before its solved, I'll know who to hunt down."

Gloriana buzzed around him. "I promise I'll handle this. I'm so sorry it even happened in the first place. I'll be more critical about who I let book here in the future. We'll have this sorted—"

"That's enough." The disdain in his sneer filled the entry hall. "Murders happen. Your job is to keep this place clean, both physically and reputationally. You haven't let me down yet, but you're close. Make sure this gets sorted out before I come by tomorrow, or else I'll begin the process of looking for a new innkeeper."

"No," she begged, "please, please. I couldn't stand to leave this place. I will sort it out. I promise. I'll handle it."

He didn't spare her another look as he opened the door and walked back out into the night.

"And not a moment too soon," said Nora. "I was just thinking how those table legs would make a perfect stake. I thought we might have another murder here tonight if he didn't leave."

Gloriana was not amused.

When there was another knock on the door, the innkeeper looked like she might have an aneurysm. "Who is it now?" she demanded before flinging open the door.

"Bad timing?" said the hulking man on the doorstep. "Oh wait, I just passed Sebastian as he was leaving. Of course, it's bad timing."

Nora waved to the newcomer. "Thanks for coming, Darius. Come on in."

Darius Pine, the leader of the Eastwind werebears had a much kinder smile than I'd imagined. From what Dante had told me about his kind, they liked to fight, and perhaps for that reason, I imagined someone much gruffer looking as their top dog. Or rather, top bear.

"He's here for Astaire," Nora explained. "The elf didn't want to stay here any longer—no offense to your lovely inn—and he can't go back to Avalon yet."

Darius strolled in, stomping snow off his boots on the welcome mat. "I agreed to let him stay in one of my cabins until he could return home. Where is he, by the way?"

Gloriana didn't seem particularly happy that these plans had been made without her consent, but she motioned upstairs. "I believe he's still in the study." She offered quick directions to the room.

Nora leaned toward Darius, adding, "I hope I don't have to spell out why we need to make sure he doesn't leave the cabin without supervision."

Darius shook his head quickly. "No, you don't have to explain to me why the husband of a murdered woman needs to stick around. I'll personally lead the watch on his front door, and when I have other business to attend to, I'll have Sandra take over. She's the most reliable person in the clan, and I know she won't fall asleep on the job."

Nora leaned forward, "And if you could exercise some discretion about—"

Darius held up a massive open palm. "Say no more. He'll feel like a guest, not someone in custody." Once Nora appeared satisfied, Darius turned to me, grinning. "You must be Dahlia." I allowed my hand to be swallowed up in a handshake. "Shaking seems too formal, frankly. I've heard so much about you from Dante that I feel like you're one of the clan. Will I be seeing you at the solstice feast?"

"Oh. Um, I don't know."

"He invited you, didn't he? I told him he should, and he said he had. If he was lying..."

"No, no," I said quickly. "He invited me. I just don't know yet if I'll make it."

He arched his brows amusedly. "Other plans?" Then, "Oh, you're probably doing something with Nora and Tanner, aren't you?"

Oh boy. Could it get any more awkward?

But Nora didn't seem to notice. "Tanner and I are just cooking a big meal. Dahlia's welcome, of course, but if I were her, I'd opt for a werebear party any day."

Darius opened his arms wide. "Then come! All three of you! And bring Ruby, if you want. She's a long-time friend of the clan. She helped Dax Banderfield with a few unfortunate situations back before he retired. There's always room enough at our table."

Nora looked at me. "Guess that's decided, huh?"

I forced a smile. I should've been happy, but for some reason, the invitation only made me feel like more of an outsider in this big, happy town. A stray along the side of the road to be adopted.

"Great," said Darius. "I'll send the details to your house once I can get Astaire settled." He shivered suddenly, rolling his shoulders back and scanning the entry hall. "Whoa, I just got a hit of something."

Gloriana huffed. "It's in your mind. Or maybe it's your sign to get your prisoner and go."

Darius clenched and unclenched his hands. "Whatever it is, I'll be glad to leave."

If a smaller person had said those words to Gloriana's face, she might've responded differently, but perhaps in light of not only his size but his status, she stayed silent. I could feel the hostility coming from her.

Darius had only expressed openly what the rest of us had discussed privately, though. I'd been in this place so long by then, I'd almost grown numb to the feel of it. I didn't particularly like that idea. When I'd first entered the manor, the feeling of it had been so strong and unpleasant. Not something I wanted to get used to.

Perhaps Nora was thinking along the same lines, because as Darius went upstairs to find his guest (or prisoner, depending on how you looked at it), Nora said, "There's still more to be done, but I think we ought to break for a quick dinner, don't you?"

I nodded.

Gloriana started with, "I'll get Wayne to fix something up for—"

"No, no," said Nora. "I would hate to put him out like that. We'll just go grab something from town. Be back soon." And before Gloriana could say another thing about it, Nora shoved my coat at me and hurried me out the front door.

Chapter Eleven

A wave of relief rolled in on the cold wind, and the icy air on my face felt like beautiful freedom. Nora waited until we were almost all the way back to the main path leading away from the manor before speaking. "I had to take a break from that place," she said.

"Oh my god, me too."

We both laughed.

"I hope you don't mind me accepting Darius's invitation," she said. "I figured you wanted to go but didn't want to offend me and Tanner by not joining us."

"No, it wasn't like that."

"For the record," she added. "We're always happy to have you around. Always. I mean, there's some time each night where we would prefer the privacy,"—I felt my cheeks warm—"but holidays, evenings—consider yourself an automatic invite, okay?"

"Thanks."

I was grateful when she changed the subject by asking, "What are you in the mood for?"

I shrugged. "Something simple." I covertly checked the coins in my coat pocket and was pretty sure I had enough on me for a meal.

Fresh snow was falling, and there was nothing so magical as the downy flakes drifting dreamily like a prolonged hush through the forest trees at night. The moon was out and reflected gently off the drifts, creating an easy runway along the path to follow without needing additional light.

When we emerged from the forest, the twinkling lights of Eastwind's center lay ahead of us. The wagon-wheel layout of the streets gave the impression of a giant wreath below us as we descended Fluke Mountain.

Nora took me to a café I'd not yet been to, a little bistro, really, where a mug of warm tomato soup and a fresh baguette with melted cheese was entirely affordable. Once we were seated with our meal, I cupped my hands around the soup mug to finish thawing them and took in the delicious smell of tomato, basil, and freshly baked bread. Life only got better once I dipped my baguette into the soup and took my first bite.

When I moaned, Nora chuckled. "One of the many things I like about you, Dahlia. You know how to enjoy the simple pleasures."

"I'd hardly call this a simple pleasure," I responded around a mouthful. "This seems like something a king and queen would've eaten centuries ago. It's *decadent*."

"I won't argue there. I wish I could say that I enjoyed the simple pleasures before I came to Eastwind, but that would be a lie. I was a chef and restaurateur. I prided myself on having refined taste and only enjoying complex dishes." She took a large bite of her meal—a sourdough roll with a mug of chicken and rice soup. Now it was her turn to moan involuntarily. "I'm so glad I got over myself," she said. "This really is incredible."

Gratitude for the meal in front of me warmed my chest as I felt more of the negative haze of Muscoff Manor leave my body.

"Who do you think Haven meant?" Nora asked, and I knew what she was referring to. I was also happy to talk about it, now that I felt like myself again.

"Not sure. We know it was a he, though."

"Ted? Someone in the house?" she suggested.

"Wait! She said he was coming and then ran away. Not a few moments later, guess who arrived."

Nora paused, her roll hovering above her soup. "Ah, true. That's interesting. Could she have been talking about Malavic? I've certainly wanted to leave a place as soon as he arrives."

"But would she know he was coming? Do ghosts know that stuff?"

"Depends on what you mean by 'that stuff.' They don't gain any sort of prophetic powers when they die, as far as I've seen. But they do sense things differently. I don't know if she would be able to, say, sense Malavic's undeadness. But perhaps she was outside prior to you bumping into her and saw him walking up the path to the manor. That still doesn't answer the question of why she would be afraid of him. You know, outside of why anyone with an intact survival instinct would be afraid of a vampire."

"Do ghost have survival instincts?" I asked.

"No," she said, "not in the way we do. But sometimes the fears they carry around in life transfer through to their death. And occasionally you meet one who doesn't know they're dead, which means they're still running around, trying to stay alive."

"That's sort of sad," I said.

Nora shrugged. "I guess, but really, death itself isn't so bad. I mean, look at us! We did all right for ourselves on the other side. Who's to say that what's waiting for people in the place where Ted leads them isn't just as much of an improvement?"

I'd have to think about that. I'd always associated sadness with death, but maybe that was a faulty belief.

"It's certainly sad for many of the people left behind," she added. "No one likes to say goodbye. And no one likes big changes, either. For the person who passes, death is little more than a change of venue."

"So, you're not afraid of death?" I asked.

Nora chuckled darkly. "No, I still am. Holding a philosophy in your mind and actually believing it with your heart and body are two different things. Plus, I love my life here. I don't want to be anywhere Tanner is not. I've tried that, and I wasn't a fan." She finished off her roll then leaned back in her chair. "I feel a thousand percent better being out of that place, don't you?"

"Ten thousand percent. What is going on there?"

"I wish I could tell you. Some places have a taint to them, though. I've just never experienced one that oppressive. I soaked it up. I felt it inside of my skin. Not just feeling bad but feeling bad about myself." She blinked. "It was strange."

"I felt the same. Oh boy, the negative things I was saying to myself in there. I thought it was just me speaking, but maybe not."

"I think it was the manor. We should probably not believe everything we think and feel while we're in there."

"That makes an investigation tricky."

"True, but now that we've put words to it, maybe we'll be more prepared to handle it. Even still, we should grab ourselves a little more protection against it."

We finished up our meal, which I was truly sad to see go, and then stepped back out into the cold. But instead of walking toward Fluke Mountain, Nora led us toward the heart of town. "Ezra's Outfitters isn't far, and if he can't help us, we can head to the Pixie Mixie. Stella Lytefoot is usually good for a powerful potion that does the trick."

Townsfolk waved to us as we passed them on the street. None seemed aware that a woman had died just outside of town. Perhaps we still had time to clean up the mess.

"We still need to speak with Wayne. Is that all?" she said.

"We haven't gotten a full timeline from Gloriana either," I said.

"True. There's certainly something a little off about her isn't there?"

"Not as much as there is with her familiar."

Nora grimaced. "Not everyone is as lucky with their familiars as we are. Speaking of which, Grim and Atlas might have to be rolled out of Medium Rare if they haven't already been kicked out by Bryant. Maybe we should go get them." She paused, frowning. "That's all the way across town, though. Ah, well, they'll learn their lesson about overeating one of these days, even if I don't teach them today."

She was right that it would be a big diversion from our route, but my heart ached being away from Atlas for so long today. I hoped he was doing okay and feeling safe.

We turned down a side street that connected to a broader avenue. Ezra's Magical Outfitters had a clean glass exterior that allowed for passersby to admire all the treasures within. If this were New Orleans, that glass would've been broken on a weekly basis, but I suspected that wouldn't happen here. Not because people in East-wind were somehow better than people in my old realm —the murders clearly proved they could be just as criminal—but because someone like Ezra would have the awareness and know-how to load up the glass with wards. No one would be reckless enough to try to break this glass. At least I hoped not.

Glowing, golden letters on the sign above the door twinkled like fairy lights as we approached. For all I knew, they *were* fairy lights.

A bell above the door rang pleasantly as Nora and I entered. The place was warm and bright inside, and I paused to take it all in. I hadn't been here before, though I'd heard all about it. Once I learned that a wand was essentially useless for me, I had no reason to come by. It wasn't like I had money to blow.

Speaking of money, these objects looked expensive. Even though our meal had been affordable, there was little chance I could purchase whatever Ezra recommended for us.

I smiled anyway as Ezra looked up from where he

stood behind the counter and greeted us warmly. "What a pleasure to see you both!"

An older woman was with him, and it wasn't until she turned toward us that I realized it was Ruby. Her eyes shot open. "Fang's sake!" she shouted, grabbing a large smoking sage bundle from the counter and practically sprinting toward us. A thick trail of smoke formed in her wake.

"Whoa, whoa," said Nora, taking a step back, holding out her hands to keep Ruby from running straight into her.

"Hold still!" insisted the gray-haired woman. She started with Nora, smudging the air all around her, and then started on me.

Waving the cloud of smoke away from her face, Nora said, "I don't remember ordering an exorcism."

"It shouldn't come to that," said Ruby, "but it might."

I coughed as the sage passed just beneath my nose and I inhaled too much of it at once.

"Good," said Ruby, "cough it out of you."

"Cough *what* out of us?" Nora demanded, taking a few more steps away from the cloud.

"Good goddess," she said, finishing with me and then turning to Ezra. "Did you not see that the moment they came in?"

He shrugged.

She shook her head. "I haven't seen such a dark cloud around two people in a long time. Where the hell have you two been hanging out today, Malavic's personal steam room?"

"He has a personal steam room?" Nora asked.

"And how would you know about that?" Ezra added.

Ruby waved him away. "Oh please. Save that. Where have you two been?"

"Muscoff Manor Inn," I said.

She looked at me confused. "That abandoned place on the mountain?"

"It's not abandoned anymore," said Nora. "It's a luxury retreat now. Sheriff Bloom is there at this very minute, lounging in a robe and slippers, and reading some romance you recommended to her."

"*Witching Hour Whispers?*"

"No," I said, "*His Sinful Wings.*"

"Oooh, that's a good one." Ruby paused. "I suppose she needed a change from Veris Bluff. That's her usual vacation spot, though I'm sure she'd appreciate it if that bit of information didn't get around. Muscoff Manor Inn. Hmm... Who runs it?"

"Gloriana Drawforth," I said. "She says she knows you from A New Leaf."

"Ah," Ruby said, dryly. "I know of her, sure. She's the one with that mangled old tabby, isn't she?"

"That's the one," said Nora.

Ruby looked us up and down again. "And where did you pick up that black cloud?"

"It was probably the inn," Nora said. "It felt off the moment we stepped inside. If you went to the place, you'd know."

"If that's where you picked up the aural gunk, I will *not* be going to that place to find out for myself. Siren's song, that was quite something. I don't think you ought to go back. Whatever it was seemed to like you two. You especially," she added, addressing me.

"Unfortunately, we don't have much of a choice,"

Nora replied. "One of the guests was found dead earlier today. We suspect a murder."

Ruby frowned. "I can see why law enforcement alone wouldn't be enough. Tanner and Stu are more than competent, but you might be up against something powerful there."

"That's why we came in," Nora replied. "For some extra protection. Though the sage attack was a pleasant start. You give all your customers this VIP treatment, Ezra?"

He grinned. "No, but I should start. I'll see if I have room in the budget for a full-time employee."

"It would certainly help keep her out of trouble," Nora said.

"Interesting to hear you're worried about *me* getting into trouble," said Ruby, "when you two walked in here looking like two black-magic chimney stacks. You said Gabby was staying there?"

"Yes, but she's not helping with the investigation."

"As well she shouldn't," said Ruby. "She's on vacation. But I do find it interesting that she would pick a place that carried anything dark like what was stuck to you. Anywhere else you might've picked up that darkness today?"

Nora and I exchanged a look, and I shook my head. "I've only been to Time to Kiln, Muscoff Manor, and a couple of restaurants to eat."

"Same," said Nora. "I suppose we could've picked it up somewhere else."

"Here," said Ezra, walking over to a display case, lifting the lid, and grabbing two objects. "When you go back there, take these."

He handed Nora and me each a single beautiful white feather. I turned it over in my hand and noticed threads of silver and gold among the snowy white that glistened under the warm lights above us. I knew what kind of feather this was right away and felt deeply comforted by it.

However, Nora was less than thrilled. "Good goddess, Ezra. Tell me you didn't steal these from the sheriff when she had her back turned to you." She narrowed her eyes at Ruby. "Did you have something to do with this?"

"Heavens, no," Ruby replied, suppressing a laugh. "What kind of a friend would I be if I stole her feathers the second she turned her back?"

"Angel feathers must be freely given to have any value at all," Ezra explained. "These aren't Gabby Bloom's. They're from an acquaintance of mine back in Avalon. She offers me a few each year out of the goodness of her heart."

My stomach clenched. These sounded like a rarity, which meant there was little chance I could afford it. I did feel much clearer merely holding it in my hand, though. It would be a shame to have to go on without it now.

"Sounds like a good profit margin," Nora said. "You get it for free, then you sell it for, what?"

Ezra shot a glance toward Ruby, who was staring a hole through him, then said, "You know what? I think in touching those feathers just now some of the generosity of my friend has worn off on me. You two take them. Just keep them close and out of sight. Darkness abhors the angelic. Whatever is there in Muscoff Manor would be wise to stay away from anyone who has an angel feather tucked on them somewhere."

Nora looked genuinely surprised. "Wow. You're really giving them to us?"

He grinned. "Consider it the generosity of the season. Happy early Solstice. May light shine through the darkness."

The approving gaze his act of charity earned him from Ruby was clearly more of a payment than either Nora or I could offer him. She sidled up to him and hooked her arm through his. "What's gotten into you?" she muttered. "Whatever it is, I like it."

He clutched her arm to his body. "I've been spending too much time with you lately, my dear death witch. You've made me more awake to life."

As their attention focused in on one another, it was clearly our cue to give them some alone time. We left Ezra's Magical Outfitters, returning into the cold night on our way back to Muscoff Manor.

And this time, we had protection.

Chapter Twelve

The timeline Gloriana offered us as we sat with her in one of the unoccupied sitting rooms was coherent enough. No large gaps in it. She claimed to have been going over the next day's menu with Wayne in the kitchen when Florian came and found her to tell her what had happened. We'd have to confirm that with Wayne when we spoke with him, of course.

Unfortunately, there was a lot of Gloriana's timeline that simply couldn't be confirmed, since she floated through the manor, going about her daily tasks silently. No one could verify most of her story. But that was the nature of her work, so I didn't find it suspicious, necessarily. If I'd been questioned by the police back in New Orleans as a suspect in a murder, I certainly wouldn't have had an airtight alibi ready. I could go for an entire day without anyone noticing me. Most people measured the quality of a housecleaner by her ability to go unnoticed and stay out of the way. Thankfully, I'd never been at the wrong place at the wrong time and had to prove where I was and when.

So, I had some sympathy for Gloriana in that regard. Don't get me wrong, I would never choose to spend time with her outside of this investigation, but I understood how being overlooked like she was could make a person feel agitated.

I shifted in my chair where Nora and I sat with her in the dining room, feeling the angel feather brush up against my back. I'd tucked it into my belt, hiding it under my shirt. Ezra clearly knew his stuff, because I hadn't felt a bit of the oppressive energy this time when Nora and I re-entered the manor. It was like someone had hit the mute button on it. The place just felt like a regular inn now, no grayness included.

My mind felt much clearer as a result, and once Nora finished her questions and let Gloriana get back to her duties, she turned to me and said, "What do you think?"

"I didn't hear anything that really stood out."

"Me neither. But let me rephrase the question: What do you feel?"

"Oh." I blinked. It hadn't occurred to me that the overwhelming emotions I'd been picking up on from others hadn't prickled my awareness at all during the interview with Gloriana. I hadn't noticed their absence. I had to think about Nora's question. "I felt a little tired when she was talking about how her day starts at four a.m. But maybe that was just normal sympathy. And then, when she mentioned seeing Haven's body upstairs, I could feel a little bit of... well, I don't know what it was, exactly. Just an intense energy. Fear, I suppose."

Nora frowned. "Hmm... You think it could be the feather?"

"I don't know what else it would be. I do feel a little stifled. But... I don't know that I want to remove it."

"No, I don't think you should. Better to be a little numb in a place like this than oversensitive."

Remembering what had happened when I removed my staurolite, I couldn't help but agree.

"We'll work around it," she said, standing. "No big deal. I've solved cases without empathy before, and I can do it again."

We found Wayne right where Gloriana had told us he would be: toiling away in the kitchen. He was cleaning dishes from that evening's dinner, and muttering to himself in a language I didn't recognize. His bright red hair stood out against the bland colors of the large kitchen, and as we approached, I realized he was standing on a stool so that he could be tall enough to reach the sink.

I'd encountered enough leprechauns around Eastwind to know that he was one without needing to ask. It was an interesting development, though, since Haven showed no signs of physical injury leading to her death. Leprechauns, like witches, possessed invisible magic, but I didn't know precisely what kind. Was he powerful enough to commit murder?

Then I remembered that Gloriana said she was with him in the kitchen when Haven was likely killed. Could she be providing *him* with a fake alibi?

Gee, Dahlia, maybe try talking to the guy before you start suspecting him of murder.

Right.

While I was disappointed to not get a read on his emotions while I had the feather on me, his stooped body language and muttering provided some clues as to his mental and emotional state.

"Wayne?" Nora said.

He jerked his head up and cowered. "Oh, miss, I'm so sorry, but it seems you and your friend are lost. This is not a place for guests. I would hate to imagine you dirtying up your nice clothes. Please, return to the rest of the house, and I can serve you whatever you need shortly."

"We're not guests," Nora said, moving closer.

He carefully set a piece of fine china on a drying cloth and wiped his hands on the stained cotton apron he wore. "You're not? Who are you?"

"We're helping Gloriana solve the murder that took place here."

Wayne lowered his head and moaned. He didn't look old enough for how big the hump on the back of his neck was. "Oh misery! Oh, tears of heaven! It is a tragedy. We have failed to protect a guest! It is the ultimate shame!"

I couldn't keep from cringing at his display.

"Now, now," Nora said, cautiously getting within arm's reach of the man and patting him just below the hump. "Murder happens sometimes. We can't go blaming ourselves for not stopping it if we didn't do anything to cause it."

"You're too kind," said Wayne. "I don't deserve it.

Look at me, blubbering away here while you attempt to comfort me. I'm the one supposed to be serving you, not the other way 'round. Your compassion brings me to tears, miss…"

"Nora."

"Miss Nora. Wait." His eyes grew large. "Not Miss Nora Ashcroft, yea?"

Nora confirmed with a "the same" smile.

"Ye put one of my cousins away years ago. Seamus Shaw. Got him locked up for taking gold from the treasury!"

For a moment, I thought our conversation with him was dead in the water, but then he added. "Scumbag, that one. You did us all a great service, putting him where he belongs in Ironhelm. You're a true servant, you are. Oh, I wish I could be as good a one as you, but here I am, letting guests get killed."

"To be fair," said Nora, "it was also under Gloriana's watch. Maybe—"

"Please don't blame her," he said, wringing his hands on his apron. "Please don't blame the innkeep. She does the best she can, yea? She does amazing. She was born for this, and it shows. I was born for *this*"—he gestured to the dishes in front of him, some drying, some soaking, and others piled up dirty beside the wash basin— "and I'm terrible at it. All I was made to do was serve, and I'm rubbish at it. She pays me too much, you know. Way too much. What does someone like me need money for? She's too gracious. She lets me eat some of the food I cook, so I'm always fed. I live in my ancestral home in Erin Park and even get a chance to go back there and water the plants sometimes. She's too generous. And I've failed her."

I looked at Nora to see if she understood what was happening here any better than I did. Judging by the way she was squinting at him, I guessed not.

"You know what would be a great service to us?" Nora said, and Wayne's ears perked up. I mean literally. His ears were quite expressive. The tips had thus far been flopped like a sad hound, but upon the word "service" exiting Nora's lips, his ears rose to sharp points. His eyes glistened as he waited for her to continue. "If you told us where you were when you found out about Haven."

"Oh, the misery," he moaned. "The death! So tragic!"

I considered myself, sometimes to my detriment, someone without an aggressive bone in her body, but in that moment, I felt like a slap to Wayne's face might be the most helpful thing I could do. Not a hard one, just enough to snap him out of this shame spiral. Or maybe I could splash some cold sink water onto him. One of my old roommates used a spray bottle to train her cat not to jump on the counters. Splashing Wayne could work a little like that.

"Wayne. *Wayne.*" Nora gripped him hard on the shoulder. "Do you want to be of service or not?"

I was glad to see I wasn't the only one thinking about getting physical with the guy.

The leprechaun pulled himself together, moderately. "Yes, of course. Always. I was built to serve."

"Tell us where you were when you found out about Haven's death."

"I was in the kitchen, miss. Just over there." He pointed to a corner. "Chopping carrots for lunch."

"And were you alone?"

"No, no. Miss Gloriana had come in here to yell at me for being slow."

"She was yelling at you?" I said, not being able to hide my surprise.

"Of course she was. I would expect nothing less. She was right. I was being slow. I was two minutes behind the set schedule. I needed to get the carrots finished and move onto the glazing. I should've already done it. But I'd had a mighty thirst earlier, and so I went out to the well to get a drink. I oughtn't have done it. It put me behind."

"I guess you never really know what happens behind the scenes," muttered Nora. "And then what happened?"

"That witch came running in. The chubby pale one. He said there'd been a death."

"And you're sure Gloriana was with you at that point?"

He nodded.

"And how long had she been back here... yelling at you?"

He considered it. "A few minutes. Three. I think it was three minutes. Oh, I wish I could offer you more accuracy!"

Nora winced. "Thank you, Wayne. We'll let you get back to the dishes so Gloriana doesn't lay into you again."

I was glad to leave the kitchen and step back into the dining room.

"Read anything in there?" she asked, once the door to the kitchen had closed behind us.

"Besides the abusive relationship he has with his employer?"

"And himself," she added. "I got a sense he didn't need Gloriana or anyone else to yell at him for him to be miserable. That's one thing Eastwind has an unfortunate *lack* of: shrinks. A good therapist could clean up here. Sheesh."

My mind shifted to the feather tucked in my belt. "I almost wish I could've accessed what he was feeling."

"Really? It seemed terrible."

"Well, sure," I said, "but what if it was an act? Criticizing yourself loudly can be a way of keeping *others* from thinking critically of you. You preempt it, sort of, and then everyone feels so bad for you, they don't want to add to it."

Nora tilted her head to the side. "Huh. You're right. Hey, maybe you can be Eastwind's first shrink."

I laughed. "I don't exactly have a license to practice."

"Perfect. None needed here."

As we walked into the entry hall, Nora said, "I had this idea when we were back in Ezra's shop. Not even a hunch, really, just a... I don't know. Intuition. Very nebulous."

"What is it?" I asked.

"I don't want to say yet. I think I need a visit to the library, though. Have you been there yet?"

"No! But I've been wanting to go."

"Then come with. I'll give you a quick tour, introduce you to the librarians."

It was strange, but my excitement to get my first visit felt like it was running up against a brick wall. I opened my mouth to say "let's go," but I couldn't get the words out. Something was giving me contrary directions. "I think... I think I should stay here."

"Stay? Here?"

As soon as I'd said it, I felt a rightness about it inside me. "Yes. I want to stay here. You go to the library. I can get more of a look around, see if I run into Haven again. There's no point in having two people working on this if we don't ever split up."

Nora narrowed her eyes at me. "I don't know. Do you think—"

"Heaven's harp!" came a voice behind me. I turned to see Sheriff Bloom leaning up against the door frame that connected the parlor to the hall. "You want to train someone or not, Ashcroft?"

Nora's mouth hung open.

Bloom held up her hands. "I'm sorry, I couldn't keep my mouth shut about this. Do you think your husband got as good at the job as he is by me keeping him glued to my side like a familiar?" She seemed to notice the absence of our two hellhounds, then added, "Closer than some familiars, I suppose. The point is that you can't train someone for the real thing by keeping them within arm's reach all the time."

Nora looked like a child being called out by the teacher, her shoulders hunched slightly. "You're right." She raised her hands in surrender. "You always are, Sheriff. Okay then. I'll go to the library, and you can stay here, Dahlia." She regained her composure as she addressed the angel. "If anything happens to her while I'm gone, this is on you."

Bloom rolled her eyes. "I'm off duty."

"What about that lecture?"

"Ah, lecturing is more of a hobby than a professional requirement." She smiled and waved her fingers to send Nora on her way.

Nora shook her head, but seemed in good humor about it as she grabbed her coat, said, "I hope your intuition here is right," and left.

Chapter Thirteen

As soon as the door closed and the reality that I was now on my own in this strange manor hit, I felt a little foolish. Maybe the impulse to stay had no sense to it whatsoever. Nora had called it intuition, but how could I be sure? I had no practical idea of what I would do now, no actions to take that I knew about.

Thankfully, I wasn't completely on my own. "Dahlia, why don't you join me in the parlor? I have a pot of herbal tea and an extra cup with your name on it."

Sheriff Bloom, while striking me as kind, was the type of person whose invitation felt like less of a suggestion and more of an order. I doubted she meant for it to be that way; she just had a confidence to her words that made me believe she knew best.

I followed her into the parlor, where she settled into a wing-backed chair by the fire, and I took the one across from her. She poured me some tea. I thanked her.

"Connecting with your intuition and recognizing when others are connecting with theirs, are two different skills," she began. "I'm glad you listened to yours. I don't know what will come of it, but every time we say yes to that part of ourselves, it feels more comfortable speaking up. Ruby has some of the best intuition I've seen in a mortal, and Nora isn't far behind. You have the gift, but you'll need to develop it before it can save your life reliably."

"Mortals?" I asked. "Does that mean...?"

Bloom smiled. "Yes. I have the privilege of being immortal. Came straight from Heaven. Much prefer Eastwind, though. The realm of Heaven isn't what most people think it is. Angels have egos, too. Eastwind works at a much more comfortable pace. More humility to be found here in general, too."

I sipped my tea, allowing the spices to settle on my tongue before I swallowed it down. It tasted like Christmas.

"Can I ask you something personal?" I said.

She seemed pleased. "Of course."

"Why did you come to what's normally a couple's retreat to spend your vacation time? Gloriana said you didn't check in with anyone."

She smiled furtively. "Ah, but I am here with someone. Someone I've had a deep, intimate relationship with my whole life. The only person who truly understands me and loves me unconditionally: me."

"It doesn't bother you to see other people with their partners when you're alone?"

"Bother me? No, not at all. I see people *hurting* each other all the time. I much prefer seeing people love each other." She settled further into her seat and crossed one leg over the other. "I suspect I'd make a lousy partner at this point, and I don't say that disparagingly. I have friends, good friends. But with few exceptions, every one of them will die. I've had to become everything I need in a partner for myself. I meet my own emotional needs. I show myself acts of service and buy myself gifts. I'm happy to report that it took hundreds of years, but I finally made it. I enjoy friendship and company, but there's nothing I need from anyone, let alone a monogamous partner. If I want a vacation, I take myself on a vacation. If I want flowers, I buy myself flowers. If I need a compliment, I pay myself a compliment."

I blinked. "Wait. What room are you staying in?"

The angel arched a brow at me. "How very forward of you."

It took a second for me to catch her insinuation. "Oh no, I didn't mean—"

"I know," she said, chuckling. "Room B."

Ah. Of course. "Did you order yourself flowers from Time to Kiln today?"

"Yes, I did. I figured you were supposed to bring them but got distracted by the murder. It's okay. I get distracted by murder, too."

"No, I did bring them!" I insisted. "I brought them earlier. There was a mystery around who the flowers were from and who they were to because there were no names listed for either in the order."

Bloom shrugged. "Why would there be? I already knew who they were from."

"But you're not staying in Room D. The flowers said they were for Room D."

"The order I sent listed Room B, but you wouldn't be the first to accuse me of having sloppy handwriting."

I could see how the letters could be confused if jotted quickly.

"The flowers are still by Room D if you want them. I heard Haven and Astaire arguing in the room when I dropped them off, so I set the vase to the side of the door, in case someone stormed out."

Bloom appeared impressed. "Good forethought there. I'll be sure to grab them when I head back upstairs."

"I would hate for you not to get full credit for sending yourself flowers," I said. "Next time you're in the doghouse with yourself, it might be a good thing to bring up."

She grinned and stared wistfully out a window where frost clouded the corners. "I might someday try romance with someone else. Just for the thrill of it. I've had some fun with it in the past. But for now, I'm content. I'm whole and satisfied. The only thing missing from my life was time spent deeply with myself, which is why I'm here. But... it looks as though this vacation might be a bit of a bust, what with the murder and everything."

"Yeah, sorry about that. If you want to get back to your reading..."

"Tanner tells me you've been spending a lot of time with Dante Fontaine."

The tea nearly dribbled out of my mouth. Tanner knew about Dante? Tanner *talked to the sheriff about my personal life?*

Bloom laughed. "You didn't know the sheriff's office was a gossip hotspot, did you? Information is safety. Violence almost always springs from intimate connections—or broken ones. The more we know about who spends time with whom, the sooner we can spot potentially dangerous patterns."

"You think Dante might be dangerous?"

"Ah. No. Not at all. The gossip about the two of you was just for fun." She winked. "Information is safety, but sometimes it's also entertainment. You don't know how boring all the paperwork of the job can be. Mountains of it. Sometimes I think about starting an avalanche so it'll bury me once and for all, and then I remember that I can't die." She sighed. "That's life. Hearing about the younger generations in town reminds me of some of my own youthful indiscretions, though, and takes my mind off the drudgery. I've gained too much wisdom to make the kinds of reckless decisions I used to, but I still get great enjoyment from hearing about others making them.

"Why I bring up Dante is because I thought you might like to hear from an impartial source who is intimately knowledgeable about the criminal element in this town that Dante Fontaine is a wonderful person who comes from a great family that raised him right. I know he's gotten into a few scuffles, but there *is* a righteous way to fight. Even violence can be done with a non-violent heart. He has a non-violent heart. I thought you ought to hear that as often as possible." She sipped her tea.

"Uh, thanks. But are you only telling me that to make something happen between me and him so you have more sheriff's department gossip?"

Bloom threw her head back and laughed. "You're much more perceptive than I thought! I won't say that was the sole purpose of sharing with you, but it certainly is something I look forward to hearing more about. Of course, if you wish to practice being in a relationship with yourself, I understand that, too. My dear friend Ruby chose that path, and it's served her well."

"Ruby True? Isn't she in a relationship with Ezra?"

"That's a question for her to answer, because I really don't know. Their connection is... long and complicated. They clearly enjoy each other's company, but if she considers herself in a relationship with Ezra Ares, then she is polyamorous, because she is *definitely* in a relationship with herself as well. And I believe she would put that relationship first, if she ever had to choose. Come to think of it, she already has, multiple times." She paused and eyed me over the rim of her cup. "Glad to see you enjoy the town gossip as much as I do. But we're not the only ones. Someone is watching us, listening in."

I felt chills run through me. "Who?"

"I don't know. You'll have to tell me. I can only feel them. I can't see them like you can."

It clicked what she was talking about, and I turned and spotted the eavesdropper immediately. "Haven," I said.

"Oh interesting," muttered Bloom before picking up her book and opening it to the bookmarked page.

Haven pressed a finger to her lips to shush me. "He's coming," she said.

"Who?" I demanded. I was done guessing. Just spell it out for me, for goodness sake!

"I don't know his name." She gasped and retreated to the corner again, her ghostly form pressed against the wallpaper, disappearing into it in places. Out of the corner of my eye, something passed by the doorway. A dark silhouette.

I didn't like this at all. It was getting *seriously* creepy.

If my conscience allowed me to opt out, I would've. Then again, what else did I expect a haunted hotel to be like?

I looked over my shoulder and saw Bloom reading quietly by the fire. She turned the page with a grin.

Her calmness steadied me. She clearly knew something ghostly was afoot, but it didn't bother her enough to interrupt her reading pleasure. Perhaps I could take the same calm approach. For all I knew, spirits couldn't touch me.

I rolled my shoulders back. Maybe my sense of calm confidence could help Haven find some courage. "Who was that?"

"I don't know," she said. "But I don't like him. Not one bit."

"Was that a spirit I just saw?"

"I don't know what he is."

I nodded. "Okay, you stay here. Stay near Sheriff Bloom. I'll investigate what that was."

I stepped out of the parlor into the entryway just in time to see the silhouette disappear around a corner, down a hallway I hadn't been in. "Hey, wait!" I called, but it didn't reappear, so I followed it.

It could be anything, I assured myself. *Just because it was dark doesn't mean it was bad. All kinds of dark things are good. Grim, chocolate, Ted, the night sky...*

I caught another glimpse of the shadow as it turned a corner at the end of this hallway. I was having serious déjà vu from the Lindley House in New Orleans, where a shadow had essentially lured me to my death, but I tried not to think about it. That situation turned out fine in the end, anyway. It brought me here. Hopefully this wouldn't end with me ending up in another realm, though. I was really starting to love Eastwind.

When I turned the next corner, I nearly ran right into someone. Someone smaller than me. "You?" I said, blinking.

"Me?" said Wayne. He held a feather duster in his hand.

"Were you walking down the hall just now?" I asked.

His eyes crossed slightly. "No miss. I was standing right here, dusting this bust of old Muscoff." I could hardly make out the features of the bronze bust on the pedestal beside Wayne. Why didn't the leprechaun turn on a light to work? "Miss Gloriana has me do the dusting in the evening, once dinner is complete and cleaned, and breakfast prep has been completed."

I was inclined to believe that the dark figure wasn't Wayne based off height alone; it had seemed much taller than the leprechaun's frame in the few glances I got of it.

"Did you see someone else walk by just now?"

He shook his head. "Why? Someone go missing?"

"No. I thought I saw someone walking this way." I frowned, my suspicions that it didn't have a corporal body all but confirmed. Wayne wouldn't have seen a spirit.

The thing had definitely turned the corner and would've walked right past Wayne, though; so either he was lying, which I wasn't sure he was capable of doing, or he couldn't see it.

I sighed. "Fang's sake." Not wanting to miss out on a golden opportunity to get to the bottom of this mystery, I reached behind me and pulled out the feather. I offered it to Wayne. "Hold onto this for me, would you? And don't use it to dust. It's more valuable than that." He blinked at the white feather which glowed gently in the dark hallway. "I know what that is! Lucky charm!"

"Take it," I said. "Hold onto it for me."

"I couldn't possibly, miss."

Not wanting to lose my window of opportunity, I shoved it at him.

He undoubtedly reacted the moment the thing left my grip and entered his, but I couldn't focus on the precise details, because the transition from having its protection to being without it was far too profound.

My head swam, and I felt the grayness of the place crash in on me. I'd forgotten how negative this place felt during my brief break from it.

A depressive sensation settled like humidity on my skin, and I felt as if I'd instantly gained fifteen pounds. The first step was a labor, but I continued putting one foot in front of the other, heading in the direction the shadow must have taken.

This hallway had three doors leading off from it. The first two were locked. The third was not only unlocked, but slightly ajar. I checked over my shoulder. Wayne had disappeared. I was alone.

I pressed open the door, wincing against the loud creak of the hinges. Outside of a dim oil lamp on a sconce by the door, moonlight streaming in between closed shutter slats was the only illumination in the space. It was enough for me to see that this was some sort of portrait gallery I'd entered.

I grabbed the lamp from the sconce, taking it with me further in. It would be difficult to spot a shadow in a room full of shadows, especially if the shadow didn't want to be seen.

I approached one of the portraits. A stern elven face stared back, his eyes gazing at something over my head, far in the distance.

My guess at who this portrait depicted was confirmed when I caught sight of the small metal marker: Linton Muscoff. The previous owner of Muscoff Manor who died alone in this place long before it was renovated. I moved to the next portrait, and it was of him as well. Were any of these of other people?

Then I realized: of course not. He was all alone. Who else would the portraits be of?

The walls were covered in a peach-colored wallpaper with delicate, painted vines weaving around it, and as I moved to the third portrait, I noticed a dark paint splatter disrupting the pattern. I held up the lamp and realized the paint splatter spelled out words: *Alone. All alone. Always alone.*

I took a step back to see more of the writing, and that's when something dark moved at the edge of the lamplight. I turned quickly toward it.

This time, the silhouette didn't elude me. "Linton," I said. "Mr. Muscoff."

The figure stared back at me. "I know you," he said.

I stood up straighter. "You do?"

"Yes. I recognize loneliness when I see it, and you are all alone."

I felt the truth in my chest, as his words spread through me like a poison.

There's a reason you're alone, I heard the voice in my head say. *You don't deserve to be with others. You're an outsider, a spare part.* The voice was the same one I always heard. It sounded like me.

"You don't belong in Eastwind any more than I do," he said.

He's right. You know he is. You've known it since you arrived. There's no point in arguing.

There was no point. He knew it, and I knew it. He was right.

But then a second voice—also me—spoke up.

He's wrong. You belong in Eastwind. Don't listen to him.

This new voice rang so clearly, I almost didn't recognize it as coming from inside of me. Even though both voices sounded like me, they didn't sound the same.

The encouragement of the new voice was enough for me to remember where I was and what I was doing. "Why are you still here?" I asked. "If you're lonely, you should go with Ted. Let him take you to the other side. I've heard it's better there. The opposite of lonely."

"I tried," he said. Had this figure stood up straight, he easily would've been a foot taller than me, but instead he hunched. I stepped closer, feeling a strange desire to comfort him.

"I left the manor after death," he said. "I wanted to return to Avalon. And I did. I traveled all the way there."

"Why did you come back?"

He shook his head. "I didn't want to. I didn't want to come back."

"Then why did you?" I insisted.

The response came not from Linton, but from a woman in the doorway behind me. "I called him back."

I turned, holding up the lamp, and saw Gloriana's

expression glowing. The harsh shadows didn't hide the glee and satisfaction on her face as she stood in the doorway.

Blocking my exit.

"Why would you call him back?" I asked. Everything in my body was telling me to run, but I couldn't. Not with her blocking the doorway. I took a shuffled step away from her instead, so that I didn't have my back to either her or Linton. I obviously didn't trust either of them to have my best interest in mind at this point.

"He won't be moving on," Gloriana said plainly. "So don't even think about pulling your death witch tricks to banish him. Linton is my soul mate."

"Huh?" I was so, so lost now. None of this made sense. "Did you know him before he died?"

"Not while he was alive, no."

"I don't understand," I said. My mind was swirling, trying to fit any two pieces of this strange puzzle together. Meanwhile, my body had all the clarity it needed to know I was cornered.

"I'm surprised you're struggling with this basic concept," she said. "Haven't you ever felt lonely, Dahlia?"

"Of course."

"Then you know. The rest of the world doesn't understand the deep sense of being utterly alone. They feel connected, part of something. People like Linton and me—and you—we know what it feels like to be a spare part. Unwanted. Not belonging to anyone or anything."

Just then, Givens the tabby bolted through the doorway, halting in front of Gloriana to hiss at me.

"You have Givens, though," I said. "Don't you feel less lonely with your familiar around?" I thought of Atlas and the haze in my mind parted. Through it, I could see his big, dopey face and feel his soft fur on my hand. Atlas would be with me until the end. He and I never had to be apart.

An aching sadness settled in my bones that he wasn't here with me.

"My familiar does nothing to cure the loneliness I feel," she spat.

I immediately felt sorry for Givens. To be paired with a witch who didn't care about him as deeply as I cared about Atlas... and I'd only been with him for a few weeks!

"The only consolation," she continued, "is that he's just as lonely as I am. There's nothing worse than being around people who don't understand what it means to feel separate from the world. Linton understands, though. I knew that the moment I entered his home. That's why I conjured him. That's why he lives here with me now."

Conjure? I didn't like the sound of that. I thought only Fifth Winds could harness spirit magic. Gloriana was some other kind, and if she was messing around in magics that didn't belong to her, things could be ugly indeed.

"He's growing more powerful," she said, grinning. "The more connections between others that he severs, the stronger he grows. It's why I advertise this place as a couple's retreat. Strong bonds between partners are like a feast for him. He can feed on them as he pleases, and he does. Each bite makes him stronger. So strong, in fact, that he can now appear to the living when they're in an elevated emotional state, isn't that right?"

The insinuation clicked immediately, and my jaw

dropped open. "You?" I said, staring at the dark silhouette. "Were you involved in Haven's death?"

"Involved?" cackled Gloriana. "He's responsible for it! I heard Haven and Astaire arguing on my way to the kitchen and sent him up there to feed. I had no idea he could manifest like that, though. I've seen him through our magic bond, so I can tell you, he's not a pretty sight when he's preparing to eat. His mouth opens unnaturally wide, and it's all teeth. He scared that elf right to death, didn't you, Linton?"

The dark thing grinned, and I got a look at some of those teeth. Not pretty.

"Haven must've opened the door, and there he was. I don't suppose he's hungry yet after *that* feast, but soon enough he'll have the proper appetite for her spirit lurking around here, and then he can finish the job."

"Gloriana," I said, trying to sound calm (and not doing a great job of it), "I can tell you're lonely. And I get it. I'm lonely too. A lot. But this is... this is *madness*. Making other people lonelier won't make you less so."

"Don't you think I know that?" she snapped. "I'll never feel like everyone else. I've been trying my whole life and never succeeded."

"There is still a way," I said. "You may not see it yet, but as long as you're alive, there's hope."

She sneered at me. "Cute. Is that what you tell yourself? That someday you'll be accepted and loved? That someday you won't fall right back into the yawning maw of loneliness that could swallow you whole? Please. Your *hope* is a cruelty. It leads you on. Give it up and your life will be better. There's no hope for you. You're like me, one of the spares. I can tell."

"No," I said, "I'm not." But her words felt like a knife to my heart.

"I enjoy what Linton and I have going on here. It's one of the few things in this life I've ever enjoyed. I have no plans of stopping it. And since you now know about it, and I can't have you telling the other death witch..."

I knew where she was going with this. My time to escape was running out.

"No one will miss you," she said. "Those are the murders that are the easiest to get away with. Nobody cares enough to bother solving them. Your death won't fill Linton like Haven's did, but it might not be a bad midnight snack."

I shot a look at the dark spirit in the corner, and he grinned. Had he looked that fearsome in life? So much about him looked fundamentally different from the other two ghosts I'd met, but I didn't understand why.

Hopefully, there'd be time to consider it later. For now, I needed to get the heck out of this portrait room.

I conjured an image of Atlas in my mind to give me courage, and then I charged straight at Gloriana. She wasn't expecting it out of me, and I caught her by surprise. But only for a second. Her reaction was quicker than *I'd* expected from an older witch like her. It was quick enough to do the job.

Her wand was out in a flash. I hardly had time to register it before its spell hit me. I flew backward, and in doing so, the chain to my staurolite pendant snapped, and the protection fell away from me.

I landed on my back but paid the pain of it no mind as the weight of Muscoff Manor came crashing in on me. At first the loathing, grief, and hopelessness was outside of me, pressing down like a pile of rubble trying to crush me beneath its weight.

And then it was inside of me.

This is how you deserve to go. Alone. Just like in New Orleans. Nobody there is mourning you. You died and nobody cared. The world kept going on. The same will happen here. Your life doesn't matter, so why should your death?

I couldn't fight back against myself. The words rushed through me, each of them feeling like an inevitable tide I'd been holding off for too long. But it was here. It was always on its way to me. Every thought to the contrary I'd ever had was an attempt to fool myself. But this, this was truth. I would die here, and that was the most I could have hoped for. I would become trapped in this house, a part of its curse, absorbed into the walls and forgotten.

And what will happen to Atlas?

This voice rang out like a bell, cutting through the fog.

What will happen to Atlas if you give up here?

I could see his big fluffy head as he lowered it into my lap. He'd been so afraid I'd bop him when we first met, but not anymore. I was a safe place for him. He loved me.

And I loved him.

He'll be fine. Nora will take care of him, replied my other voice. *He'll be happier that way.*

I heard someone scream "No!" before realizing it was me.

No! I want to care for him! I don't want to leave him! I love him!

The oppressive grayness ejected from me like a

shockwave. My vision cleared, and Gloriana was thrown backward by the force and went thudding awkwardly against the doorframe. Givens screeched as he was knocked off his feet and tossed into the hallway.

My body ached as I pushed myself to my feet, preparing as best I could for her next strike.

But it didn't come. She made no move to cast another spell my way. Instead, she remained on her back, moaning slightly.

I searched for Linton and found him a dark huddled mass in the corner. He was gripping his knees to his chest and quivering.

Quivering? In fear? Of whom, me? Surely not. I wasn't sure what I'd just managed to do, but it hadn't felt at all scary to me. It had felt like freedom.

A guttural sound pulled my attention back to Gloriana. At first I couldn't understand what I was hearing, and then it registered. She was crying. Not just crying—absolutely blubbering. I couldn't make out any particular words through the rest of her involuntary noises.

One more thing became clear: she was no longer blocking my way! I could make a break for it! I could escape!

So why wouldn't my feet move?

Shouts from the hallway drew my attention. "It's a wraith! Dahlia, it's a— fangs and claws!" Nora skidded to a stop just inside the door. She looked from Gloriana to me. "What the hellhound?" And then her attention moved to Linton in the corner and she cursed again and rushed toward him, chanting in a language I didn't know. He whimpered as she continued, but he didn't fight back.

"No!" said Gloriana, her blubbering subsiding. "Don't hurt him!"

"Enough out of you," said another voice. Bloom appeared in the doorway, shrugged off her robe, which not only revealed lavender striped pajamas underneath, but freed up her movement, allowing her to shoot shimmery gold cuffs from her palms. They wound around Gloriana's wrists, binding her hands in front of her body.

The innkeeper began blubbering again.

Nora shouted a few final words, and then there was the sound of a minor explosion, and Linton vanished in a puff of the same smokey substance of which he was made.

Even Gloriana fell silent when that happened. It felt like there was no choice. The stifling presence of Muscoff Manor vanished with him.

The room was silent. I gratefully sucked crisp air into my lungs.

I was safe.

"There's always next year for a relaxing vacation," said Sheriff Bloom, yanking Gloriana to her feet. "I suppose this one's over, seeing as how the innkeeper is about to be arrested for murder."

"I didn't do it!" Gloriana insisted, sniffling obstinately. "It was *that* thing! You saw it, didn't you? That ghastly thing."

"The wraith might've caused Haven's death," Nora replied, "but you conjured it."

"It's not that simple!" Gloriana protested.

"That's okay," Bloom said. "Juries can handle complicated." And then the angel pushed her out of the portrait room.

"You okay?" Nora asked, looking me up and down. As she approached to check me over, the toe of her boot knocked into something, sending it skittering across the floor. My staurolite. She went and picked it up. "Siren's song, Dahl. Did you take them on without this?"

I tried not to get too excited at the nickname. I'd never had one. "I didn't mean to. It just came off."

She handed it over. One of the tiny links in the chain had broken apart. I wouldn't be able to put it back together myself.

"Ezra can fix that for you in half a second. Come on, we'll head over there."

"Can it wait a little bit?" I asked. "I'd kind of like to find Atlas."

Nora smiled. "Yeah, it can wait. Let's see if he's in a bacon coma, passed out in a back alley with Grim somewhere."

Chapter Fourteen

I slept like the dead. The real dead, not the kind that come back to haunt manors. When I woke up the next morning, Atlas was still snoozing, snoring gently, his back pressed against my side. I didn't want to wake him yet. No point in doing so anyway; I didn't have to be at work for hours.

Atlas kicked his legs, dreaming that he was running or maybe doing a jig with the leprechauns. Anybody's guess. I carefully turned toward him and slipped an arm around his big, shaggy body. I was growing used to the natural smell of his fur. I buried my face between his shoulders and drifted off that way, indulging in the glorious sleep of early morning when you have no place to be and your body still feels heavy. And you have your best friend cuddled up beside you.

Atlas was the first one awake after that, and he had no issue waking me up with a jab from his wet nose. *"I'm hungry."*

He had extricated himself as little spoon and stood by

the bed, his head resting on the edge as he stared at me. I was hungry, too, so I put on some real clothes, grabbed my coat, scarf, and gloves, and we ventured outside.

It was a Saturday, and it *felt* that way. There was something in the air that said, "You made it!" Even though I felt like I'd slept in, we were still out and about early enough that the previous night's fresh powder hadn't been marred by boot prints yet. Only the go-getters were out, most of them carrying bulging canvas bags on their arms. Solstice preparations, no doubt.

As the morning sun sparkled off the snow, Atlas and I made our way to the Outskirts. A clear mental picture of my breakfast order was already forming in my mind: eggs, sausage, bacon, maybe even a pancake. *Definitely* coffee.

Atlas seemed in a good mood and hardly flinched at all when a witch came zooming by us on her broom, cutting dangerously close in front of us. I think I might've reacted more strongly than he did; one night of sleep, however sound, was not likely enough to reset my nerves after what I'd been through.

I didn't see Nora when I first walked into Medium Rare, the tinkling of the bell above the door announcing in its Pavlovian way that it was about to be chow time. The increasingly familiar sound of it lightened my spirits immediately.

Without realizing I was doing it, I looked in the corner for Ted in his usual booth. He wasn't there. I thought I knew why.

His booth was empty, despite the rest of the diner being packed. It was an unspoken rule that between certain hours, that was the reaper's booth, whether he was there or not.

The diner was crowded, but I spotted a trio of teenagers getting up to leave and hurried over to claim the open booth. I had Atlas guard the spot while I bussed the dishes from the table and brought them over to a bin behind the counter. Then I grabbed a rag and wiped the table down for myself while Bryant was busy taking orders on the other side of the dining room.

Once a housecleaner always a housecleaner, I supposed.

I didn't mind. I liked doing this sort of thing for myself rather than asking anyone else to. The Medium Rare family had been more than generous to me since I'd been in Eastwind. I ate here all the time and had only managed to pay twice, and only because I'd dropped the money on the table and dashed before anyone could do a thing about it.

Nora appeared from the kitchen, carrying a large tray stacked with breakfast foods. I'd arrived with such a clear picture of what I was going to order but seeing that breakfast burger with the egg over-easy on top next to the plate of French toast complicated my decision. I had to remind myself that there would be plenty of other mornings to come here and pig out.

Once she offloaded the tray, Nora brought over a mug of hot coffee, a small creamer pourer, and a glass of water. "You're gonna go straight for the coffee, and I don't blame you," she said, "but take it from me: what you went through last night leaves you more dehydrated than you know. Avoid the headache: drink the water first." She took a seat across from me, despite the busyness of the place. I felt Atlas shift at my feet, making some, but not much, room for Nora's legs under the table.

"You sleep okay?" she asked. "No nightmares?"

"I don't think I had a single dream last night, come to think of it. He did." I motioned to the white lump at our feet.

"*How do you know?*" he asked.

"*You were running in your sleep.*"

"If it was only *dreams* he was having last night," said Nora, "consider yourself lucky. I don't know what Atlas and Grim got into yesterday, but I kicked Grim out of the bedroom at three in the morning. I thought I might suffocate on the gas he was putting out."

Atlas solved the mystery for me: "*A toddler knocked a whole bowl of queso off the table yesterday. Grim cleaned it up.*"

I shrugged, feigning ignorance. "Yeah, anybody's guess what they got into."

"It can take a few days to process an investigation," Nora said. "Besides tying up the loose ends—Tanner is taking care of those right now, by the way—it can be difficult to wrap your head around what happened to you."

I chugged down some water. She was right. I was thirstier than I realized. "Is it weird that I don't feel the need to wrap my head around it yet?"

"It would be weird for *me*... but maybe not for you. We seem to be different in fundamental ways." Then she quickly added, "Please take that as a compliment."

"Fair enough," I said. "For what it's worth, I wouldn't mind being more like you. You... you seem to know exactly where you belong."

She leaned forward. "That's because you're seeing me years on. Trust me when I say I didn't know where the hell I belonged when I first got here. All the accomplishments I'd built like a fortress around myself back in Austin? Those didn't travel here with me. It's hard, I get it." She paused. "Do I strike you as an honest person?"

"Yes."

"Do I strike you as someone with a little bit of insight on how things work?"

"Definitely."

"Then I hope you'll believe me when I say you belong in Eastwind. You may not feel that way yet, and that's okay. But I can see it. You wouldn't be here if you didn't belong and if this place didn't need you. Don't listen to anyone who says otherwise, even if that person is you."

I nodded. "I'll try."

"Please do. But back to the investigation."

I was more than happy to change the topic. "You said Linton was a wraith. What is a wraith exactly? Is it not the same thing as a spirit?"

"It's *sort* of a spirit," she replied. "It's a dark entity, usually created in the form of someone who lived. I've only dealt with a couple of them and they don't all appear the same way. Each one has a unique way of presenting. It took me a while to pick up on it this time, but I suspected that the feeling in the house wasn't a curse so much as a presence. I went to the library to look up beings that could fill a space like that, and surprise, surprise..." She shook her head. Then, blinking, she smacked the table. "You must be starving! What can I get you?"

I explained my ordering conundrum.

"Protein and grease are what you need. I'll bring you

a plate that's going to put you right back to sleep after this."

I laughed. "I have to go into work this afternoon. I can't sleep the day away."

"Ah, no you don't. I already sent word to Raven and Jude about what transpired last night. They insisted you take today off."

"Oh!" I enjoyed my job, but a day off work, no matter what that work was, was a treat. "Great. Thanks!"

She leaned down to address Atlas. "And I haven't forgotten about you. You in the mood for a hash?"

His fluffy tail smacked the linoleum floor a few times in the affirmative.

As Nora left to put in the order, I finished off my water, mixed just the right amount of cream and sugar into my coffee, and leaned back in the booth, cradling the mug against my chest so I was treated to a rich whiff of it on each inhale. I closed my eyes, took a few more deep breaths, and then did some people-watching.

There I was, the only one at my table while others gathered with friends and family, but I didn't feel lonely.

But then again, I had Atlas with me. As long as he was with me, I wasn't alone.

Nora brought out our food, and I closed my eyes to take my first deep inhale of it as the plate clanked on the tabletop. "That was fast."

Nora shrugged. "Anton's been reading a lot of books on improving focus and productivity lately. He's rearranged all the tools around his griddle. Guess it's work—" She cut herself off just as the bell over the door rang again. I wouldn't have noticed its sound beneath the loud conversations if she hadn't stopped talking. Her expression changed completely.

I realized why when I turned my attention to the door.

Nora marched toward Count Malavic where he'd paused just inside the door and scanned the place with a snide look of superiority.

"What are you up to now?" she demanded, but he swept past her and approached my table. She hurried after him.

"How are you feeling today, Dahlia?" he asked.

I looked from Malavic to Nora and back, not sure if I'd get in trouble for answering. I went with, "Fine."

"I heard you had quite a wild night."

"Oh," said Nora, "you mean on account of that employee of yours conjuring a wraith to prey on the guests of your establishment?"

He turned calmly toward her, a look of amusement turning the corners of his lips. "Yes. That."

"Be honest with me for once, Malavic," she said. "When did you know Gloriana had conjured a wraith? Was it before the murder happened?"

His mouth fell open in shock. "Nora. After all I've done for you over these years, you would think that little of me?"

"Can it," she barked. "You've only ever done anything for anyone so that they owed you later on. When did you learn about the wraith?"

He pulled off one of his black leather gloves, revealing the pale skin of his hand. "We could discuss this all day, but why? Let's focus on the fact that the wraith is gone. And while that means I no longer have an innkeeper and must enter the choppy waters of hiring someone new, I won't hold it against you. It's only a small matter, and once I get it sorted out, I have a feeling that business at Malavic Manor Inn will really take off."

Nora's face dropped. "You did not rename it after yourself."

"Why shouldn't I? If you decided to rename this Ashcroft's Diner after all you've done to keep it running, no one would blame you. The fact that you *haven't* shows a startling lack of business savvy, frankly. When you make yourself the brand, you make yourself irreplaceable." He slipped his bare hand into his coat pocket and pulled out two brown leather pouches, shoving one into Nora's hand and setting the other one on the table in front of me. I heard the clank of metal inside of it and knew immediately what this was.

"A little something for the trouble," he said, addressing me with a smile. "No one can say I don't pay my fair share to keep this town safe. There were about twenty years where I financed the entire sheriff's budget." He grinned. "Gabby wasn't happy about it, but when people need money badly enough, they'll take it where they can get it." He bowed his head at me. "You did exceptionally well, Dahlia. I look forward to there being a competent Fifth Wind in town who doesn't hate me for no clear reason."

"No clear—" began Nora agitatedly, but he cut her off with, "Enjoy your nourishing breakfast, Dahlia!" and then he slipped his glove back on and left.

"For the record," Nora said, "I have *plenty* of clear reasons not to like him. Enough to fill a book. A whole bunch of books." She tossed her pouch of coins onto the table. "You can have these. I won't hold it against you if you accept his money."

"Oh," I said, looking at the two pouches in front of me. "I feel like I shouldn't accept it from him if he's as bad as you say."

She shook her head. "Accept it while your stomach still allows you to without revolting. You don't need to take up my cause against him. Given enough time, you'll develop your own reasons for disliking him, I'm sure. In the meantime, take the money. Donate it to charity if you'd like or spend it on something fun. Any money that doesn't go straight back into his pockets is money well spent."

She headed off to take the order of a faun family who'd just grabbed an empty table, and I returned my attention to my food. I wanted to eat it while it was still hot.

Beneath the table, I heard Atlas licking his chops. He'd already devoured his while I was distracted by Malavic.

Nora was dead-on with her breakfast recommendation, and of course she was. If anyone would know what they were talking about in this situation, it was a Fifth Wind who also owned a diner.

I was dipping the last bite of bacon in some runny egg yolk when the door to the diner opened again, and in stepped a tall, hooded figure.

Ted looked around, saw his empty corner booth, and hollered to Nora, "Thanks for saving my spot! Heh."

She shot him a quick thumbs up.

Ted hadn't arrived alone, though. At his heels was a small cat that I quickly realized was a ghost. It stayed close to the hem of his robes, following him through the crowded diner and hissing when someone scooted their seat backward and sent a chair leg through it.

"Ted's here," I said to Atlas. "And he's brought his cat. Let's go say hi."

"*I do like Ted. He never tries to bop me. But I don't know anything about his cat. What if it's mean?*"

"*Then I'll banish it,*" I replied, though I had no idea how one accomplished that and had no intention of trying. It didn't seem like a thing you'd do to your friend's pet. "Besides," I said. "It's a ghost. It's physically impossible for it to bop you on the head."

I grabbed my coffee and walked over; Atlas could follow or not, but I really wanted to speak with Ted. I had a few things to wrap up with him.

"Hi, Ted!"

When he looked up at me, his face obscured by the impenetrable shadow of his black hood, I had the strangest certainty that he was grinning. "You having a great day so far?" he asked.

"I am. And who is this?" I kneeled and offered a hand to his cat.

"That's Mudbug. It's okay, Buggy. She's a friend. And she can see you."

"*What if I don't want to be seen?*" asked the ghost cat.

"If you don't like being seen, you should meet my familiar, Atlas. He likes to hide, too. But it must be awfully lonely going around without anyone being able to see you."

"*Sometimes. But Ted takes me places where things can see me in the Deadwoods. Most of them are gentle, but*

I've had to hide under his robes a few times. Nothing in the Deadwoods will try to hurt Ted."

I smiled. "I'm glad you have such a good owner, then."

"Wait a second," said the reaper from his seat at the booth. He leaned down to look under the table, first at Mudbug and then at me. "Are you... able to speak with him?"

"Oh!" I said, realizing. How silly of me to forget! I was so carried away with being nice to Mugbug that I forgot to keep my ability to communicate with other people's familiars a secret. "Yes," I whispered under the table. "But please don't tell anyone. I'm worried the other witches would feel betrayed or jealous if they found out I could hear their familiars speak."

Ted nodded. "Your secret's safe with me."

He sat back up, and I straightened from the crouch.

"Wanna sit?" he asked.

I accepted his offer, sliding into the booth across from him. "Thanks."

"Any time. And I mean that. I don't sit here alone every day because I want to."

I nodded. "I'll join you more often, then. But sometimes I do like sitting alone."

"I understand. I like being alone in my cabin for long stretches. But not always."

"No," I said, "not always. And it feels better when it's your choice to be alone, doesn't it?"

He nodded.

"Hold on." I leaned forward as something occurred to me. "If I can talk to Mudbug, does that mean he's your familiar?"

"No. He was someone else's familiar. It didn't turn out well. He's my best friend now. I'm never alone when I'm with him. But since he's not *my* familiar, I can't speak with him. But that's okay. I know all kinds of ways to communicate. I developed a system of whistles to communicate with my phoenixes, and I've been working with Buggy on a system of purrs."

"He's not very good at it," said Mudbug from below the table. I pretended I didn't hear that and nodded along as Ted offered up a few examples of his feline language.

I can't describe how amusing it was to listen to a grim reaper do a variety of cat impressions in the corner booth of a packed diner, but suffice to say, I was riveted. So riveted that I almost forgot why I'd gone over there in the first place.

Bryant approached the table and dropped off a cup of hot coffee with only a nod before he left again. Ted reached out with his gloved hands and pulled the mug closer to him on the table.

"Why were you later than usual today?" I asked, already suspecting the reason.

"I found Haven. Or rather, she came and found me right as I was about to leave my home to come here. She wanted me to do her a favor before she agreed to come with me."

"What was that?"

"Deliver a message to her husband. She was sorry they argued. She regretted that being their last conversation."

"Oof," I replied, "I bet that was hard to get through for you."

"Not hard at all," he said. "I cried, sure, but one of the

great things about this hood is that no one can ever tell. Heh. Besides, I don't mind crying. It feels good to cry. Not every reaper is as talented at it as I am, and it catches up with them in the end."

"I guess death and crying go hand in hand," I said.

He sipped his coffee. "Yes, but maybe not in the way most people think. I don't think death itself is sad. I know people are heading to a lovely next place. All of them. Even the bad ones get another chance, and I think that's lovely, too. So, it's not sadness that makes me cry."

"What is it then?" I asked.

"It's love. Real, lasting love, the kind that exists when all the petty disagreements are blasted away."

I felt a lump forming in my throat and took a sip of coffee to swallow it down. "Do you give everyone the opportunity to have a final exchange with their loved ones?"

"No," he said. "Not everyone asks for it. And not everyone would make good use of it. Some people just want to drive in the final nail to the coffin, so to speak, and I don't like being a part of that. But I could tell Haven wasn't interested in a parting shot. She and Astaire fought because she wanted more of his attention. She loved him so much that the only time she felt safe and herself was when she was connecting with him. She told me that. She told me a lot of things this morning."

"That's nice of you to wait for people to be ready."

"I don't always. Heh. Occasionally, I can tell it's their time to go, and when it's their time, it's their time. I'm not in charge of that, and I do technically have a boss to answer to."

"You do? Who?"

"The pull of fate. I have a sense for Doom. It tells me where I need to be when I need to be there."

Nora appeared at our table. "And it's a real buzzkill." She set down a plate in front of him. "You speak with Astaire this morning?"

"Sure did."

"And how's he doing?"

Ted shrugged. "You can probably guess. Darius Pine took great care of him, though. Astaire is heading back to Avalon today, so at least he's ready enough to go home. That's something."

"I guess so," said Nora, refilling my coffee mug with the coffee pot in her hand. "Tanner said Gloriana's not saying much while she sits in jail."

"I hope her punishment isn't too severe," I said.

Nora looked at me with surprise. "You do? You know she wanted to kill you, right? And she's responsible for conjuring the wraith that killed Haven."

"I know," I said, staring at my coffee. "I probably shouldn't feel that way. But I do. When you think about it, it takes a very lonely person to do something that awful. I sort of feel bad for her."

Nora grunted. "I see your point, and maybe I'm just getting old or jaded, but she had her familiar. She had people around her just like the rest of us. And we're not out there conjuring wraiths to ruin the connections of those around us." She sighed. "Yeah, I think I am getting jaded, now that I hear myself say that. Or maybe I just need some more coffee." She left Ted and me to make a round through the tables, using the coffee pot in her hand to refill cups at each stop.

"I think it's very kind of you to feel that way," said

Ted. "I sometimes struggle to connect with people even when they're right across the table from me. Heh. People like Gloriana—and most of the murderers I've met— needed help somewhere along the way that they never got. It's too bad."

"It is," I said.

"Maybe it can be a reminder to the rest of us to go out of our way to connect with people who feel alone."

I grinned across the table at the reaper. "I think that's a lovely takeaway, Ted."

Epilogue

I could hear the party going on inside the cabin as Atlas and I stood on the front step. The snow-flecked wind whistled through the trees at our back. What we were waiting for was me to get some freaking nerve. We were there at Darius's home, and so close, but there was still a chance for me to decide that this was a dumb idea and bail. Until I knocked on the door to announce us, that little voice in my head had the opportunity to convince me that I'd only been invited out of pity and that no one really cared if I showed up or not. And if no one cared whether or not I showed up, then I could hurry home and save myself the embarrassment of figuring out too late that I was definitely intruding, and everyone had hoped I wouldn't actually come.

"*I smell ham,*" said Atlas, interrupting my thoughts.

In the days leading up to this, I'd talked Atlas through all of *his* phobias about attending a large party with mostly strangers. In the end, the promise of scraps, which

Grim had gotten him addicted to, was enough to give my sweet, scared boy the courage to stay by my side.

I couldn't chicken out if *he* was mustering this much bravery.

I knocked three times… then remembered Ruby's rule and added a fourth.

All doubt about the sincerity of my invitation melted away when Dante opened the door with the broadest smile I'd ever seen on him. "Dahlia! I'm so glad to see you! I was worried you would skip out."

"Never," I said. And then, to my shock and pleasure, he reached through the doorway and pulled me into a hug. "Happy Solstice," he muttered into my hair. When he let me go, I stumbled a little, weak in the knees.

"It's too cold outside. Get in here." Dante stepped aside, and Atlas nudged me ahead of him and through the doorway.

The inside of Darius Pine's large log-cabin home was warmly lit with candles around the walls and magical glowing balls of light in every corner.

And now I smelled ham, too. And spices. Was somebody mulling wine?

"Come on," said Dante. "I'll introduce you to everyone."

My stomach dropped at the word "everyone," and I thought, yet again, about quietly disappearing. *What's the point of all this?* said the rude little voice inside me. *They won't even bother remembering your name.*

"Just be warned," he said, "they're going to try to embarrass me. I'm the youngest of my family and making me blush is their favorite pastime."

"You blush?" I asked, laughing despite myself.

He took my coat. "Of course not. I'm shameless. They *try* to make me blush, but they haven't succeeded yet." He hung up my coat. "Oh, and by the way, my great uncle Pete is... his mind doesn't work like it used to. When I told him a Fifth Wind was coming, he got his mind set on you being able to, uh, see the future. I told him that's not something Fifth Winds can do." Then his brow furrowed. "Or wait, it's *not* something you can do, right?"

"Not as far as I know. But wait." I pressed two fingers to each temple and shut my eyes tight. "Maybe..." Then I let my hands fall and opened my eyes again, shrugging. "Nope. Nothing."

He laughed. "Just checking. Well, Pete thinks you can, so he's going to ask you for some predictions. Feel free to make up anything you want if you don't feel like explaining to him thirty times that you can't see the future." He placed a hand on my back and guided me in the direction of the living room. Right before we emerged into the gathering, he said, "I really am glad you came out, Dahlia."

My heart fluttered, and then suddenly the room exploded into loud cheers.

To welcome... me?

I caught a glimpse of Atlas's white tail just before it slipped out of view the way we'd come. I didn't blame him. I felt like running away from all the attention, too. But I didn't. I stayed right where I was, smiled, and waved. "Hello. Happy Winter Solstice. Thanks for letting me join you."

"Where's your familiar?" came a voice from the crowd. "I heard he's completely white. I have some ham set aside for him."

"That's my brother William," Dante explained quietly to me.

"If you have ham, he'll be back," I said. "He just takes a little bit to warm up."

Darius Pine emerged from the kitchen, carrying two crystal glasses with a rich berry-colored liquid in them. He handed one to an older woman who thanked him with a nod before returning to her conversation and then made his way directly over to us. "Dahlia, I'm glad you came. I just saw Atlas hiding under the dining room table."

"Oh dear," I muttered, embarrassed for his behavior. "I promise he won't eat off the table. He knows better."

"I wouldn't be so sure," Darius replied jovially. "I've heard he's been spending a lot of time with Grim. That hellhound has a way of influencing others into mischief. Sometimes of the criminal variety."

I nodded. "I'll keep a close eye on him. Thanks again for letting me come. I know having a witch around probably puts a damper on the werebear fun."

Darius jerked his head back. "Are you kidding me? Not at all! I see these people every day. It's nice to have a fresh face around. I'm not new to this town, of course. I know some weres are biased about witches, but I don't tolerate those attitudes in my clan. I used to have a witch living up here in the cabins. Nobody could ever say a bad word about Eva, though. She was nothing but kind and generous."

I perked up. Eva—Angelina to me—had lived with the werebears? I'd had no idea. It turned out that she had done more than I knew to pave the way for my life in Eastwind. I could feel her presence here even though she was a realm away. I'd had no idea of the friend I had in her until I left New Orleans.

I looked around the room, trying to spot other familiar faces. I did recognize Dante's uncle Ansel and aunt Jane, and I wondered briefly if Ansel had finished the book he'd been reading when we saw him at Whirligig's Garden Center. Probably best not to inquire.

Grace said she, Landon, and Monte would swing by toward the end of the night, once they had given proper face time to family. I was looking forward to knowing someone else here.

"Nora and Tanner still coming?" asked Darius Pine.

"They said so. They were just running a bit behind. Grim and Monster were in some dispute about who was fiercest, and Nora and Tanner were trying to deescalate it before they left the house. They said they'd be over once they felt sure they wouldn't come home to a ransacked house."

Darius chuckled, and then he did something totally unexpected. He pulled me into a tight hug. Ah, so *this* was the bear hug I'd heard so much about.

When he let me go, he said, "If you don't already know, we hug around here. If you're going to be spending more time with the clan, I suggest you get used to it." He pulled a soft green wreath of woven vines and ruby-red berries from a nearby stack of them and hung it around my neck. "Happy Solstice, Dahlia."

The whole cabin felt suddenly warmer.

"I got you something," said Dante once Darius had returned to the rest of the party, leaving the two of us alone on the periphery.

My stomach dropped. "You did?"

"Don't worry, it's okay if you didn't get me anything. I'm not big on getting gifts anyway. Consider it a welcome gift more than a solstice gift. That way you don't feel like you should've gotten me something."

That did make me feel slightly better, and I was able to start guessing what the gift might be. I was drawing a serious blank, though.

"It's in the den," he said, and nodded for me to follow him out of the living room.

The den was as cozy as could be with a log burning in the fireplace and soft harp music floating through the air. I had no idea where it was coming from, but I was at peace with that.

Dante nodded for me to settle in on a small love seat, and then he grabbed a wrapped present from a pile at the foot of a yule tree and brought it over to me. He sat right next to me as he handed me the gift. "I hope you like it, but it's okay if—"

I held up a hand. "I already love it." And then I set to unwrapping it.

I gasped as I discovered what was inside of the box. "Dante. You didn't."

He grinned. "I wasn't sure if you had your own yet, but I understand every witch needs one."

I pulled out the teapot and immediately recognized it as the one he'd been working on at the studio. The glaze was gorgeous, like nothing I'd seen before. As I held it up, the colors shifted with the movement. It was purple, then it was blue, then turquoise, then gold. Each new angle revealed a gorgeous new shade.

"Do you like it?" he asked.

"Are you kidding? I love it!"

"There are two matching cups in the box, too."

I dug those out next, and they had the same incredible glaze work on them. I couldn't believe this teapot was *mine*. He'd spent all that time making it for *me*.

He helped me get the set back in the box, and then he set the box on the floor. "I'm glad you like it. Grace helped me pick out the glaze. Mostly she assured me that you would like whatever glaze I went with."

"She was right," I said. "I've never had someone make something like this for me before."

He said nothing but scooted closer to me on the couch and grinned. Then he looked toward the ceiling. I followed his gaze.

"Is that...?"

"Maybe they don't have it where you come from," he said, "but it's called mistletoe. Anyone who stands or sits under it—"

"Yes, we have the same tradition where I came from." My cheeks flushed. Should I move out from under it so he didn't feel obligated to kiss me?

Oh, but I very much *wanted* to kiss the man.

Then show some courage and kiss him already! came the clear voice inside of me.

He leaned toward me on the love seat, and I met him halfway.

I would certainly find myself feeling alone at other

times in my life, but this was not one of them. This moment was the opposite of loneliness.

Dante slipped one of his hands over mine a moment before our lips met.

The kiss was short and sweet. That was all it needed to be to make the moment feel absolutely perfect.

About the Author

Nova Nelson grew up on a steady diet of Agatha Christie novels. She loves the mind candy of cozy mysteries and has been weaving paranormal tales since she first learned handwriting. Those two loves meet in her Eastwind Witches series, and it's about time, if she does say so herself.

When she's not busy writing, she enjoys long walks with her strong-willed dogs and eating breakfast for dinner.

Say hello:
nova@novanelson.com

facebook.com/thecozycoven

instagram.com/authornovanelson

bookbub.com/authors/nova-nelson

goodreads.com/nova_nelson

amazon.com/author/novanelson

More books from Eastwind

The Eastwind Witches Cozy Mysteries

Crossing Over Easy (Book 1)

Death Metal (Book 2)

Third Knock the Charm (Book 3)

Queso de los Muertos (Book 4)

Psych-Out (Book 5)

Gone Witch (Book 6)

Love Spells Trouble (Book 7)

Storm A-Brewin' (Book 8)

Hallow's Faire in Love and War (Book 9)

Dead Witch Walking (Book 10)

Old Haunts (Book 11)

First-Realm Problems (Book 12)

Happily Hereafter (Book 13)

The Ruby True Magical Mysteries

Werebear Scare (Book 1)

Elves' Bells (Book 2)

Vampire's Ire (Book 3)

Find them here: www.eastwindwitches.com

www.ingramcontent.com/pod-product-compliance
Lightning Source LLC
Chambersburg PA
CBHW021551310726
48972CB00003B/770